Mr. DARCY'S Christmas CALENDAR

JANE ODIWE
TIME TRAVELS WITH JANE AUSTEN

MR DARCY'S CHRISTMAS CALENDAR

Copyright © 2014 Jane Odiwe

First published 2014 2014 White Soup Press

The right of Jane Odiwe to be identified as the Author of this Work has been asserted by her in accordance with the Copyright, Designs and Patents Act 1988

All characters and events in this publication, other than those clearly in the public domain, are fictitious and any resemblance to actual persons, living or dead, is purely coincidental.

All rights reserved. No part of this publication may be reproduced, stored in a retrieval system, or transmitted in any form by any means, electronic, mechanical, photocopying, recording or otherwise, without the prior permission of the publisher or a licence permitting restricted copying. In the UK, such licences are issued by the Copyright Licensing Agency, 90 Tottenham Court Road, London, W1P9HE

ISBN-13: 978-1502961068

For Sara and Olly Oll with much love,
and fond memories of Christmases past

MR DARCY'S CHRISTMAS CALENDAR

Lizzy Benson visits Jane Austen's house in Chawton, and buys a special Advent calendar in the gift shop, but strange things start to happen when she opens up the first door and finds herself back in time with all the beloved characters from her favourite book, *Pride and Prejudice*. As she finds herself increasingly drawn into an alternate reality, Lizzy discovers not only is Mr Darcy missing from the plot, but also that Jane Austen has never heard of him. All Lizzy can hope is that she can help to get the story and her own complicated love life back on track before Christmas is over, and bring everything to a happy resolution in Jane Austen's imaginary world!

Jane Odiwe comes to it steeped in Austen, in all her renditions; Odiwe's sentences often glint with reflections of the great Jane ... - HISTORICAL NOVEL SOCIETY

Chapter I

Door Number *One*

It really did look like a Christmas card. The red brick house glowed with yellow light through frosted windowpanes brightening the gloom of the wintry day. Lizzy wrinkled her nose as feathers of snow tickled her face and settled like iced stars on her scarlet beret. It had been a bit of a nightmare to find it: a train, a bus ride, and a twelve-minute walk along snow-covered lanes, but now she considered it had all been worth it. Jane Austen's house buried in the countryside village of Chawton couldn't have been more perfect to Lizzy's eyes. Perhaps deciding to visit the house in the middle of winter hadn't been her brightest idea, but there was no denying her excitement. Lizzy felt a sense of anticipation, the house looked enchanted as if under a fairy spell, and she half wondered if she might bump into Jane herself at the door.

Finding the entrance at a barn door by the side of the building Lizzy soon realised it was locked, and it occurred to her then that despite all appearances the house might not be open. Looking up, dizzying spirals of snowflakes whirled through the air making her blink, and for the first time she prayed that the snow that was settling in high drifts might stop. Setting off that morning in fine weather Lizzy hadn't even considered the house might be closed or that there might be a problem getting home. The snow was totally unexpected, and though she loved to see it, Lizzy felt a little anxious now she saw it continue to fall. She wondered if perhaps she should head back along the lane to the bus stop when, to her great surprise, she heard the sound of a door opening. From the main building opposite the head of a tall man peered round the glass-paned door.

'Look, we're really short-staffed. No one's turned up, and to be honest, I thought no one in their right mind would come today. I assume you're here to see the house?'

Lizzy nodded. She saw a cross-looking young man in his late twenties with a mane of dark, almost black hair waving back from a face of strong features. She heard a public school accent, confident but with more than a suggestion of arrogance, the kind her father would be terribly impressed by. His dark eyes, to match his unruly curls, were boring into hers as if he hated the very sight of her. Unable to meet them, she was overwhelmed by a sense of rising panic whilst simultaneously thinking she'd never met anyone so rude. He hadn't even said hello.

'I've come from London,' said Lizzy. 'It's taken me a while to get here, but I suppose if you're closed, there's not much I can do.'

'No, we're shut. Cassandra's might give you a cup of tea, I suppose.'

Lizzy had a strange thought he was talking about Jane Austen's sister for a minute until she remembered that the café across the way shared the same name.

'No, they're closed, too,' she said.

The sign for the café had been a welcome sight on the way as she'd trudged up the road, but she'd known with a sinking heart that it was closed before she'd even reached it. As Lizzy waited for him to speak again, she heard the crunch of footsteps in the snow behind her.

'I'm here now, Mr Williams, you can get back in the warm. I'll open up!' cried a cheerful voice.

Lizzy turned to see a lady with a pleasant face advancing gingerly towards her, picking up her long skirts to avoid getting them wet. Dressed from head to foot in Regency costume she appeared to be totally at home in her clothes, and Lizzy supposed it must be a kind of uniform she wore when showing people round the house.

'Come in out of the cold, dear. I am sorry I couldn't have been here sooner, but what with the weather and I know not what to tell you about first, I am in quite a dither this morning. My nerves are apt to plague me, but you'll forgive me for running on so. Mr Williams would have attended you in any case, I am sure.'

The door opposite resounded with a loud bang as it shut. Mr Williams disappeared.

Lizzy didn't like to say that the rude man had told her to go home, and decided to say nothing. In a way, she hoped he might see her and she felt a certain satisfaction in knowing that she'd got what she wanted, after all. Following the lady into the barn, Lizzy blinked as the bright strip lights were flicked on in the shop.

'Do make yourself at home, dear. I'll just make sure everything is in order in the main house so have a look round at your leisure. My youngest daughter was here yesterday, and though a delightful companion, she is inclined to be untidy. I daresay the dining room table will be littered with bonnets and ribbon, but that's my Lydia — never happier than when she's pulling apart a hat and making it her own.'

She reminded Lizzy of Mrs Bennet especially when she laughed like a young girl, her curls trembling as she disappeared through a door at the end. Lizzy suppressed a desire to giggle, and wondered how the lady managed to keep up her way of talking, as if she'd just stepped out of a Jane Austen novel.

Lizzy looked around at the wealth of books and gifts in the shop, most of which she longed to own. The shelves were lined with the books Jane Austen had written and revised in the very house she was about to see, and there were mugs and bags, bookmarks and fridge magnets to tempt the pennies out of her purse. On the counter was a pile of Advent calendars with a scene like the one she'd witnessed earlier. A painting of Jane's house in the snow was sprinkled with twenty four windows to be opened during the festive season, some of which lay exactly over the place where the real windows were situated, over the doors, or were hidden in the snow-clad trees and sky. Lizzy was just making up her mind to treat herself to one when the lady came back.

'Oh, my dear, you've made an excellent choice, and one you won't regret, I'm sure,' she said, and as Lizzy took out her purse to pay for it, the lady added, 'Don't trouble yourself about paying for it now. There's time enough to do that later. Now, if you'll just go into the changing room, you'll find it all much more enjoyable if you put on your costume first.'

Before she could ask any questions the door was opened for her, and when Lizzy stepped inside the small cubicle she found a day dress and scarlet pelisse hanging up, along with a plain chemise, half-boots, and a fur trimmed bonnet with green satin ribbons. She'd always wanted to try on a Regency costume, and this one looked so authentic that she thought it would be fun to wear. Lizzy was soon dressed, the outfit was quite easy to wear and more comfortable than she'd thought it might be, fitting her to perfection, as if it had been made with her in mind. A glance across at the looking glass showed an image of a young woman she hardly recognised looking quite wide-eyed with astonishment.

When Lizzy emerged rather cautiously, the lady clapped her hands. 'Oh, my dear, you look better than I dreamed possible. Scarlet is very becoming on you, and the green ribbon brings out your hazel eyes. Now, don't forget your calendar. Please take it with you, and, as it's December the first today, you should make haste, and open number one!'

Encouraged by the lady's enthusiasm Lizzy carefully tore round the perforated edge of the window and peeled it back. She'd never grown out of the childish excitement of having an Advent calendar, and this was extra special. Behind a beautiful gothic window the picture gave a glimpse of the room itself. There on a chaise longue lay a pink satin bonnet.

'That means you must go to the drawing room first,' said the lady. 'Look for the signs and you'll soon find it.'

Lizzy picked up her bag, and clutching the calendar set off around the back of the house following the path until she came to a white door. The thought that this was a doorway through which Jane had passed many times was thrilling, and turning the handle she crossed the threshold with a reverent step.

'Lord, is that you, Kitty?' came a shrill voice. 'I thought you were never coming home!'

The room Lizzy entered was strewn with ribbons and lace, yards of satin and silk flowers covering every surface and tumbling onto the floor. A young girl seated on the chaise longue looked up expectantly.

'Oh! I thought you were Kitty, but I suppose you must be here for one of my sisters, though I have to say you look as if you've just stepped out of my mother's monthly magazine, and are not at all the sort of plain girl they usually keep for company.'

Apart from being completely taken aback at the sight and manner of the girl who looked just like an image from an illustrated edition of Jane Austen's novels, Lizzy couldn't think what she was talking about.

'I'm so sorry,' Lizzy began, 'but I was told to come here.'

'And I expect that person was a round plump lady who talks too much and quivers like a jelly not quite set. My mother! Lord knows she cannot help herself, but she will interfere. You're not the first and I daresay you will not be the last. However, do not be alarmed. I am delighted you are here. You can help me trim this wretched bonnet. I cannot do a thing with it! Tell me, what do you think of this ribbon?'

Before Lizzy managed to speak the young girl spoke again. 'Are you here for Jane or Elizabeth? I expect they're closeted away somewhere telling their secrets to one another. I am not interested in their dull tales. Anyway, I have a secret of my own. I shall tell you if you like.'

Based on what she'd seen so far of her companion, Lizzy decided she wouldn't be required to say much at all but something told her to be on her guard.

'I don't think...'

'Good, I knew you would want to hear it. I know Miss Austen doesn't like it when we peep, but I cannot help wanting to know what will happen next. All I wished for is to have our dreary cousin taken away, but I know there is much better in store. I've seen the very manuscript she's working on!'

'Miss Austen?'

'Of course Miss Austen! Miss Jane Austen, the one who owns this very house. At least, her brother Edward really owns it but Miss Jane and her sister Miss Cassandra live here with their mother.'

'Miss Jane Austen is here in this house?' asked Lizzy, hardly able to believe her ears.

'Yes, of course, she's in the next room where she sits scribbling on her little pieces of paper about us all. I should be vexed for it has to be said she can be very unkind about me, but she has promised to send me to Brighton, so she's not all bad, by any means. I heard her say it out loud, and I cannot wait!'

Lizzy was sure her suspicions were correct. She'd visited houses and museums in the past where actors were employed to play the parts of historical figures, but she'd never seen anything quite so real or convincing. The girl who was clearly brilliant at role-playing must be acting the part of Lydia Bennet, and the lady in the shop was performing very convincingly as her mother, Mrs Bennet. It all made sense now.

'Do you think I could see Miss Austen?' Lizzy asked.

Lydia looked doubtful. 'She may see you, but then again, she may not like to be disturbed. Miss Austen keeps the door hinges deliberately unoiled, so she can hear the door squeaking when she is about to be intruded upon. You will soon find out if you go beyond the door.'

Lizzy followed Lydia's pointing finger to the door ahead, which was firmly closed. 'Do you think I should? I wouldn't like to interrupt her if she's writing.'

'Only you can decide what is best. If you take a leaf from my book, nothing ever stops me from pursuing the wishes of my heart.'

Lizzy was most undecided, especially when she considered that it might not be wise to take advice from Lydia Bennet. But, surely this was all part of the exhibition, and she was being guided, even invited to go through the door. And if she didn't hurry, time would run out, and she would have to go home. Pinned to the door was a piece of card with a number two engraved in silver upon its cream-coloured surface. On closer inspection she read the words, *An Invitation to the Ball*, written in a flowing script.

Chapter 2

Door Number *Two*

Lizzy knocked and waited. To her great disappointment she heard nothing, no answering voice, not even a sound. Mustering all her courage she turned the handle feeling all the while that she really wasn't very sure if she should. Entering a narrow vestibule where a fire crackled in the hearth, another door with a glimpse of the room beyond beckoned her on. But, the sound of horses' hooves approaching outside summoned Lizzy to the window and she gazed out in amazement at an ancient carriage rumbling by, and noticed the frozen duck pond she'd somehow completely missed on the way to the house. She was just wondering about the coach, and thinking how the scene must appear little changed over the last two hundred years when she heard light footsteps not far behind her, and as she turned to go into the other room, caught sight of a dashing figure of a young woman, stealthily running up the creaking wooden boards, two at a time, disappearing upstairs to rooms out of sight. A muffled laugh sounded above, a deliciously bright and happy noise which echoed in the silence, and Lizzy couldn't help wondering if it had been Jane Austen that had made her escape, though that idea really made her chuckle. Whoever it had been, she clearly hadn't wanted to be found, yet Lizzy couldn't help feeling sorry to have missed her.

Cautiously advancing inside, she found a cheerful parlour and the delicious aroma of hot, buttered toast. A dining table and chairs occupied the centre space upon which a pot of honey, a blue and white plate bearing a few breadcrumbs with a sticky knife, and the scatterings of pretty china, consisting of a flowered teapot, a sugar box and a milk jug, were the remnants of what appeared to be a breakfast meal. A kettle hissed and steamed on a trivet over the roaring fire in the grate and on either side of the fireplace, a cupboard and a cabinet held a variety of precious treasures: miniature portraits of loved ones, beautiful teabowls, and a box of candles. Every picture was decorated with a glossy sprig of holly, and a swag of the same, entwined with ivy, was held in place on the mantle with scarlet ribbons. Set before the window a small tripod table and writing desk were placed. Lizzy was drawn to it by the sight of several leaves of paper, a bottle of ink and a quill pen, but as she approached she saw that the even handwriting in brown ink was partially hidden by a plain sheet, which had been placed on top. She tried not to stare, and though the temptation to nudge the paper slightly to reveal more was great, she knew she should not. However, she was intrigued by the words that caught her eye. *The prospect of the Chawton ball was extremely agreeable to every female of the family.* Lizzy couldn't see any more than that, and in fact, it seemed this was where the author of the piece had decided to stop writing for the time being.

She didn't quite know what to do next or where she should go, whether she should sit on one of the chairs at the side of the room. Sitting at the small writing table was out of the question. Lizzy had a feeling she knew exactly whose script flowed across the top of the paper, and besides that, the words she'd read seemed almost familiar. The prospect of a ball - it made her think of the Netherfield ball that Mr Bingley gave in *Pride and Prejudice*. Had this been left here on purpose as if Jane Austen herself had just penned the words to her famous book? Lizzy had no doubt this was all part of an elaborate entertainment put on by the museum, and she was so glad she'd decided not to go home. Standing by the window looking out at the frosty landscape, she saw two girls suddenly come into view, arm in arm, chatting and laughing, as they approached the front door. She heard their voices in the vestibule; within moments they'd entered the room still talking nineteen to the dozen, and were soon warming themselves by the fire, as bonnets and gloves were removed and outdoor capes thrown over a chair. They didn't seem to notice Lizzy who couldn't decide whether to interrupt their happy chatter and introduce herself. It was a few moments before they spotted Lizzy who was so surprised when they spoke to her that she plumped down on the little chair by the writing table.

'How do you do? You must be Lizzy, my namesake.' The lively girl who spoke these words was very pretty with dark eyes that sparkled under fine arched brows. She held her hand out, and Lizzy stood up again to take it, smiling back into the eyes that were full of humour.

'Yes, I am Lizzy Benson,' she replied, and tried to curtsey as she'd seen the Bennet sisters do in the film of *Pride and Prejudice*. 'I hope I'm not intruding.'

'Not at all,' said the other equally beautiful girl whose fair curls fell over her forehead in ringlets. 'Welcome to Chawton; we were expecting you.'

'You were expecting *me*?'

'Forgive me, my name is Jane Bennet, and we are delighted to have your company. Miss Austen loves visitors, especially those that love her books.'

'Miss Austen *knows* about *me*?' Lizzy could not believe her eyes or ears, and even though she guessed they were actors making it all up, she still felt a kind of thrilling sensation at the thought that her favourite author somehow knew about her.

'Yes, indeed,' added Elizabeth, 'and she is so pleased that you could come to Chawton. She has a lot of work to do, and would welcome your help.'

'I'm not sure how I can be of any use to her,' Lizzy replied, certain that she must now be dreaming. Was it a coincidence that these girls shared the same names as those of her favourite heroines?

'There is to be a ball at Chawton Great House,' said Elizabeth, 'and Miss Austen has yet to decide what will happen.'

'To think Mr Bingley brought the invitation himself,' Jane said. 'He is most pleasant, and gentleman-like, Miss Benson.'

'And, if that does not proclaim his very special interest in a certain young lady sitting next to me, then I will marry Mr Collins!' added Elizabeth.

'Oh, my dearest sister,' laughed Jane, 'you'd best be careful not to make such outrageous statements, for I am sure you do not wish such an attachment.'

Elizabeth laughed, throwing back her head and showing a pretty mouth. 'No, indeed! It will be quite difficult enough avoiding a dance at the Chawton ball, let alone a walk down the aisle of Chawton church.'

'But, I am certain you will not wish to avoid a certain redcoat,' said Jane, looking demurely at her hands in her lap as if butter wouldn't melt in her mouth.

'If you mean Mr Wickham, as I am sure you do, I will say that I would be quite happy to dance with that gentleman.'

'Only 'quite' happy? Eliza, you are blushing at the very sound of his name.'

'Mr Wickham may be assured of my accepting a dance ... or two, if he is lucky,' Elizabeth said. 'I must admit I am looking forward to seeing him again.'

The lady from the shop walked in then, followed by Lydia and two other girls, one who kept whispering and giggling in the latter's ear, and another whose studied concentration on a book meant that she hardly attended to the general conversation.

'I'm so pleased you've met my daughters, Miss Lizzy,' the lady said confirming that she must be playing the role of Mrs Bennet. 'Here are Kitty, and Mary to say hello to you. Now, what have you been discussing? I expect all the talk has been of the ball to come and what you are to wear.'

'Mama, I must have a new gown, I've simply outgrown all the others,' said Lydia pulling a face. 'It's not my fault I've grown so tall, and, in any case, Kitty will be pleased to have my old gown, I'm sure, it's hardly been worn.'

'But, I am older than you,' Kitty began, 'and I do not see why I should have your cast-offs just because you can't stop growing.'

'Girls, girls, please stop squabbling. We shall see what we can do this very afternoon,' said Mrs Bennet who seemed keen to stop an argument forming. 'It's too late to go into Alton even if it stops raining, but I shall ask Hill and see if we can't find something to tack onto the bottom of your gown.'

Lizzy looked to the window and was astonished to see not only had the snow stopped, but also that the sky was dark with torrential rain falling in stair rods. It didn't look as if it was stopping any time soon.

'Oh, the snow is melting at last,' she said out loud, 'I'd better think about going home,' but when there was no reaction to her outburst and they all ignored her, she almost felt as if she were sitting in the theatre and had rudely interrupted the play. More and more, the idea that she was watching a performance of her favourite book, *Pride and Prejudice*, formed in her mind. The names of the places were changed slightly to fit in with the locality, but other than that, it seemed so very similar. She had a minor part to play, and they were doing their best to include her to a small extent, but it was so well done, and the characters so real, it was as if she were really visiting Chawton cottage or Longbourn with the Bennet sisters.

Her reverie was broken by the sound of a young man's voice calling in a singsong fashion from beyond the door. 'Yoo hoo! Halloo, ladies, where are you?'

A figure in clerical black burst into the room and made a beeline for Elizabeth, sitting too closely on the sofa next to her, and asking if she'd heard the news that they were all invited to the Chawton ball.

Lizzy looked across to see Elizabeth's teasing expression with her dark brows arching high above her eyes, which sparkled with amusement. 'Mr Collins, do you intend *accepting* Mr Bingley's invitation? I imagine if you did, you might consider it improper to join in the evening's amusement.'

Lydia snorted and nudged Kitty in the ribs, as they all waited for his response.

He nodded thoughtfully for a moment or two and looked most solemn before speaking. 'Miss Eliza, I can assure you I entertain no scruple whatever on that head, and am very far from dreading a rebuke either from the Archbishop or Lady Catherine de Bourgh, by venturing to dance.'

'But, as a clergyman,' she responded, 'whose behaviour is the standard for all those in his immediate society, surely you cannot condone such revelry. Should we not abstain from such evil, as the Bible instructs us?'

'I am by no means of the opinion, I assure you,' Mr Collins continued, 'that a ball of this kind, given by a young man of character to respectable people, can have any evil tendency. I rather enjoy dancing myself, and I hope to be honoured with the hands of all my fair cousins in the course of the evening. I take this opportunity of soliciting yours, Miss Elizabeth, for the two first dances!'

Elizabeth's astonished countenance brought forth several hardly suppressed giggles from Lydia and Kitty, and several more undisguised howls of laughter as they watched their sister reluctantly accept, before she rather huffily picked up her cloak, immediately leaving the room and heading off out through the front door in rather more subdued spirits than she'd entered it. Mr Collins left soon after humming a tune and looking very pleased with himself.

'Mr Collins is very sweet on Lizzy,' said Mrs Bennet. 'Two dances - well - I can only hope it will lead to more! Come Kitty, come Lydia, we must make haste if your gowns will be finished in time.'

One by one, the others departed until Lizzy was left quite alone, not knowing whether she should burst into applause. It had been very good, but she really ought to think about getting home.

The sound of the front door shutting once more had her looking through the window for Elizabeth returning after her walk. To her great astonishment Lizzy saw somebody else. The rain had stopped and in the scene outside, large snowflakes were again falling thick and fast upon the broad shoulders of a gentleman Jane Austen would have described as tall and good-looking. A more Darcy-like figure Lizzy could not have imagined with his greatcoat flapping around him just as dramatically as Colin Firth's ever did, his smooth breeches delineating a muscular physique, and with dark hair tumbling in curls to his collar. It was only when he glanced towards the window that she cried out in surprise and recognition. Looking quite unlike the irritable man she'd met briefly before, Mr Williams stared directly into her eyes.

She heard the sound of doors opening and shutting rather loudly and the clip of boots upon the wooden boards. When the dining parlour door opened and Mr Williams entered the room, Lizzy could not have been more astonished. She was slightly tempted to laugh for he still looked rather cross but she also had to admit if anyone could pull off a gentleman's Regency outfit, it was him. It was a pity he was such an obnoxious person, he was actually quite handsome, she thought. Knowing he would only be rude if she asked him what he was dressed up for, she decided to say nothing and waited for him to speak first.

'Mrs Bennet said I'd find you here. Look, we're shutting up early, you can't stay here any longer.'

He's a silver-tongued charmer her mother would have said, she thought, but unable to be just as rude back again, she answered in a friendly way. 'Of course, I'd better be going; the weather looks to be really closing in. Anyway, I've had a lovely time, even if it's been a bit short. The entertainment has been wonderful in the rooms I've seen. Excellent acting, the characters were spot on!'

'The bus leaves in five minutes.' He was scowling at her again and checking the fob watch hanging from a grey ribbon attached to those breeches that left nothing to the imagination.

Suddenly Lizzy felt she'd had enough of being polite. Knowing he was just the sort who would never remember her even if she chose to come back again one day, Lizzy decided she wasn't going to let this pompous oaf have the last word. 'Why are you dressed like that?' she demanded. 'Oh, don't tell me, I've guessed it! You must be playing the part of Mr Collins. Yes, there's no doubt who you must be - grave, stately, and with formal manners - true to the life!'

She said it to wound, as she knew it would. Mr Williams was clearly a vain young man judging from the care he'd taken with every little detail to get his clothes and hair exactly right. She bet he thought he was the spitting image of Mr Darcy (not that anyone but Jane Austen knew what *he* looked like) and she could just imagine him at an event like the *Jane Austen Regency Week* that took place every year in Alton, where he would make sure that everyone could see and admire him. No doubt, some silly girls would be completely taken in by his appearance and she imagined him playing on it to full effect. She could hear him chatting them up with that posh voice and see them hanging on his every word.

'As a matter of fact, I'm just trying on my clothes for the Advent Ball tomorrow evening at Chawton Great House, just down the lane. Of course, it's only for privileged, invited guests. The noblest families from miles around will be gathered in celebration. Ordinarily, a ball of this kind would command a ticket of a thousand pounds apiece.'

'Why am I not surprised by that?' Lizzy retorted, feeling that to be just as rude might be the only way to communicate. 'Goodbye, Mr Williams. I hope you have a wonderful time, I expect you'll be in your element.'

She turned to go, and promptly walked into Mrs Bennet who appeared at the door as if by magic.

'Lizzy, where are you off to in such a hurry?' she demanded. 'You're not thinking of leaving us, I hope. I'm afraid the last bus has been cancelled, my dear. But, do not worry. We shall be very jolly here. You must stay, mustn't she, Mr Williams?'

Lizzy heard a sort of strangled grunt. 'She may do as she pleases.'

Mrs Bennet ignored him. 'In any case, it is all arranged, is that not so?'

'Whatever do you mean?' asked Lizzy.

Mr Williams shook his head, gave Lizzy one more look of scornful disdain and left the room.

'We cannot send you home in this dreadful weather - I would feel forever responsible! If anything happened to you, I should never live with myself. Indeed, the very thought sets my poor nerves jangling.'

'But, my mother will be so worried,' answered Lizzy quickly.

'Surely not when she discovers you've been invited to stay here, my dear. There's a telephone in the hallway. Phone your mother, but I'm very sure she can spare you.'

'I've my own phone, but I really will have to go. Besides, I've brought nothing with me. I haven't a clean change of clothes or ...'

'I'm afraid it cannot be helped,' interrupted Mrs Bennet, 'and in any case, I am sure we can find you something to wear.'

'It's not so very far to walk to Alton, if I go quickly. I can get a train from there. Perhaps I should phone for a cab.'

Lizzy reached inside her pocket for her mobile, but saw immediately on taking it out that it was completely dead. How that had happened she had no idea, she was sure it was fully charged before she left home.

'There won't be any hansoms now, my dear, there's not a carriage or conveyance to transport you anywhere and walking is quite out of the question. You would get lost in these country lanes that all look the same in the snow. And look, it's getting dark.'

There seemed to be no arguing with Mrs Bennet who took charge immediately. 'I will show you to your room first and then you can telephone home. Follow me.'

Chapter 3

Door Number *Three*

Lizzy reluctantly followed Mrs Bennet up the narrow staircase to the first floor, and just along the corridor until they stopped in front of a white painted door on which was yet another number. This time, the figure three was fashioned out of brass, and hanging below it on a hook, she saw a framed miniature painting. It was a watercolour of two girls dressed alike in simple, white muslin dresses, exquisitely painted. The girl on the left reminded her very much of the portrait of Jane Austen that Lizzy had once seen in the National Portrait Gallery, except that she looked much younger without her spinster cap. Her hair was dressed on top of her head with curls falling round her face. She was smiling with such warmth that her hazel eyes appeared to sparkle in the light. With her head inclined towards the girl next to her she held out her hand, from which were suspended three pendants on gold chains. The very pretty girl seated at her side gazed back at her with a similar look and expression. There was no doubt who she could be in Lizzy's mind and all at once, she heard a whisper which seemed to confirm what she'd guessed.

'Cass,' said a voice softly in her ear, and thinking there must be someone else behind her, Lizzy swung round. There was no one there, and Mrs Bennet, who was busy jangling keys, selected one before stepping forward to unlock the door. Leading her into a modest-sized room with a view out onto the garden, there were two canopied beds filling the room, hung with curtains in blue check. On either side of the fireplace were two cupboards, which gave tantalising glimpses of the contents within. Shelves of blue and white china on the left displayed a handsome washbowl and jug and on the opposite side the tall cupboard door had been left open showing dresses hanging neatly in a row.

'You can have the Miss Austens' room tonight,' said Mrs Bennet, taking out one of the gowns before shutting the cupboard doors. 'They won't be needing it, seeing as Cassandra is away and Jane has left already because she'll be sleeping at the Great House this evening. The sisters have always shared a room, you know. Full of secrets they are, almost as sly as my eldest girls for keeping confidences. Your namesake, Elizabeth, she's the worst of the lot! Now, Lydia is a different kettle of fish. She has no secrets from her dear mama!'

Lizzy was beginning to think that "Mrs Bennet" was taking all this play-acting a bit far. It was one thing to dress up and put on a performance for the sake of visitors to the house, but it was after closing time now. To tell the truth, it was starting to unnerve her, but she felt she couldn't really question the lady.

'I am to sleep in here? Is it allowed?' asked Lizzy.

'Well, I'm sure it is if Miss Jane requested it herself. She can be very fussy, to my way of thinking, but a bed's a bed, I say, and it does no good to be too particular!'

'Jane Austen said I could sleep in her bed?' Lizzy couldn't help herself and laughed out loud. 'Oh, now I really am in Fairyland!'

'Fairyland? No dear, you're in Chawton, just until the snow melts. I shall leave you now. The housemaid will help you undress, as I daresay Mrs Hill will be attending to my daughters. And I'm sure she'll have lots to say about what you should wear tomorrow evening.'

'What I should wear?'

'Why, you're to go to the ball. Miss Jane said you should attend with everyone else. You can go in the carriage with my girls, if the lane has been cleared in time. The men are out there now with Mr Hill, and no doubt, they'll be back again in the morning, and come back frozen to the bone. This is the worst snow we've seen since Lydia was born and that was a winter I never thought I'd survive. Not that I ever complain. As I said to Mrs Lucas, no good ever comes of grumbling, though I feel perfectly justified to complain on the subject of Mr Bingley. My poor daughter - he will keep her waiting for an announcement.'

Mrs Bennet smoothed the counterpane, muttering under her breath and shaking her head, oblivious to the fact that Lizzy was there, and she was still talking and lamenting Jane's lot as she exited and made her way down the stairs.

Lizzy looked about her now she was alone. It was a very cosy room, she saw, with a chocolate rug on the floor and striped wallpaper on the walls. A jug of holly and ivy on the windowsill before the casement gave it a festive air, the scarlet berries glistening in the candlelight. The oval looking glass above the fireplace reflected her face, pale and slightly anxious, but she was comforted by the sounds of a clock ticking and wood crackling on the fire as it burned. There were bookshelves, and Lizzy couldn't help picking up a copy of a volume of *Camilla* by Fanny Burney. She'd read once that she was one of Jane's favourite authors - what a lot of trouble the curators of the house had made to get all the details right, she thought. There were all sorts of personal objects left lying around - a pair of spectacles, a thimble and a needlecase were left neatly on the mantelshelf at one side and an ebony hand mirror, a patch box and a bottle of lavender water were arranged on the other. Two pretty reticules dangled from a wooden chair by the fire, and a piece of lace was folded over the top. On a handsome tambour desk, two Tunbridge workboxes sat on top in pride of place. The lid of the desk was rolled back and Lizzy could see the contents inside. There was a pile of music, each carefully transcribed note beautifully sketched upon fine lines, and there were several songs, she noted: *The Soldier's Adieu, Robin Adair,* and *The Yellow Hair'd Laddie,* looked well-thumbed and were covered in personal notes and alterations. A sheaf of paper in the middle of the desk looked like a manuscript file and there was a bottle of ink and a well-used pen, its feathers short and stubby. Drawn to the writing like a magnet, Lizzy tried very hard not to look and for at least a minute, she avoided reading the top page. However, like a heroine in a novel, the temptation proved too much. What she read really surprised her!

Elizabeth or Lizzy, as her family named her, had never been to a ball before. There were not funds for such gaieties and now she had been invited to such an occasion, Lizzy felt uncertain about what to do and how to behave. Young and inexperienced, with little confidence in her own style, she worried that she would make an ill-advised decision about how to be dressed. But, her friend came to the rescue in time, and loaned her a dress to wear, a gown to surpass all others she had ever possessed. To be fine, dressed in white, was a thought that pleased her, so when the maid came to help her she gave in readily to all her ministrations. There was one further concern. So few were her ornaments and jewels that she suffered an anxious moment, enough to sober her spirits even under the prospect of a ball given principally in her honour. However, on receipt of a note accompanying a jewel box in the drawer of the desk all was resolved.

Lizzy read it through twice. She had a feeling that this had been especially written for her to find. Was it a coincidence that the girl described in the passage seemed just like her? There were several small drawers in the interior of the desk. Pulling each one out a little fraction, whilst simultaneously pretending that she wasn't in the least bit curious, she almost squealed when in the very last one she discovered a slim leather box and a note addressed simply to *"Lizzy"*.

Inside was a poem.

This little trinket I hope will prove
To be not vainly made

For if you desire an ornament
It will afford you aid.

And if we ever need to part
T'will serve another end,
For when you look upon this jewel
You'll recollect your Freind.
Jane Austen 3rd December 1811

Lizzy opened the box, her fingers trembling in anticipation. She gasped when she saw its contents. Lifting the precious treasure from its box Lizzy discovered a beautiful topaz cross, suspended on a gold chain. She knew she'd seen it before and remembering the painting of the two sisters she flew to the door to take a look. There it was - her cross, along with two others that Jane held in her hand. What she hadn't noticed before was the plaque underneath which gave a little history of the painting.

This watercolour of Jane and Cassandra Austen was painted shortly after their sailor brother Charles presented them with topaz crosses bought with his prize money in 1801. There is a third cross in the painting, about which we currently have no record or information.

So, there was a little mystery about the beautiful jewel she held. Lizzy wondered if she dared try it on. Picking up the note, she read it through again looking for any clues that might tell if it was really hers to wear. What struck her as rather strange, was the date at the bottom of the poem. This note had been written almost to the day in 1811, the year that *Pride and Prejudice* had been written and revised.

Lizzy's eyes alighted on the Advent calendar she'd left on the bed. A strange light was glowing from the doors of all three, illuminating the objects within. Although she knew she hadn't opened doors two and three, she saw they were open now. December first shone with the picture of Lydia's pink bonnet, December second showed an invitation announcement, and before she'd even peeped at the door of December third, Lizzy knew exactly what she'd find. Twinkling and golden, the topaz cross and chain glittered in the eerie light looking identical to the one she now placed around her neck. It had been December first when she'd arrived at the house. How could it now be December third?

The sound of footsteps on the stairs had her darting round, but she needn't have been frightened. It was only the housemaid, Sally, come to help her settle in and see that everything was to her satisfaction.

Chapter 4

Door Number *Four*

When Lizzy awoke next morning, she couldn't think where she was at first. And then she remembered that she was lying in Jane Austen's bed, and that the whole reason she was there was because she'd bought an Advent calendar in the shop at Jane Austen's house. The memories of the day and evening before slowly returned. None of it seemed to make any sense, and the idea that she'd somehow passed into some unknown and strange reality was a growing concern. Ever since she was a little girl Lizzy had always felt there was a fine line between what she imagined and what was real. Spending a good amount of time in her imagination, whether daydreaming or in reading books meant that reality and fantasy were often blurred in her mind. But nothing had ever felt so real as the strange episode she was now experiencing. Never before had her mind co-operated quite so much with bringing to life the worlds she'd often visualised. Every detail had been thought of, but she could not think her brain quite capable of summoning up the mended patches on the curtains, or able to supply a darkening stain on the ceiling by the window where it seemed ice water was seeping in through a hole in the roof. It would probably be better if she didn't think about it too much, Lizzy decided, and she really would have to make an effort to get home today, she thought, her mother would be worried to death. But, one glimpse at the window told her there'd been no cessation in the weather. Snow was falling thick and fast, and pulling at the bedclothes to trap in the warmth, she hoped she wouldn't be stuck there for another whole day.

As she lay there familiarising herself with every last feature of the room, she heard the sound of a pianoforte being played. It must be Elizabeth or Jane practising, she thought, and Lizzy remembered reading that Jane Austen loved to play before breakfast. Whoever was playing sounded very accomplished to her ears, and the tunes were very pretty, some longer concertos, and others quite short songs. When it stopped, she decided it must be time to get up, but wasn't quite sure whether she should attempt to do that herself or wait for the maid to come in. Swinging her legs out of bed, she sat on the side and listened to the sounds of the little clock on the mantle, a soothing sound that made her feel as if she might easily be hypnotised.

Lizzy's eyes were drawn to the Advent calendar propped up against the looking glass on the dressing table. Number four was shining with a bright white light bursting from its centre like a Christmas star, and it looked far too inviting to ignore. Lizzy fetched it and opened the door, gasping when she saw the picture inside. It looked rather like her, the painting of the girl who stood observing her reflection, and the longer she stared, and the more she thought about Miss Lizzy Benson depicted in a beautiful ball gown, the more she found herself drawn into the painting. And just moments later, it was as if, like Alice in Wonderland, she'd shrunk, closed up like a telescope until small enough to pass through the tiny door, but it was done so seamlessly and swiftly, in such a blink of an eye that it was impossible to know how it had happened at all.

Lizzy admired herself in the glass. She looked just as if she'd stepped out from a period production on television, rather like Elizabeth Bennet herself, she thought gleefully. The gown was quintessentially Georgian, made of fine cambric embroidered with a panel of whitework leaves and flowers tumbling down the front and along the hem. There were puffed sleeves, cut to show off her slender arms, and a white satin sash tied at empire height made her appear tall and elegant. Her hair was twisted up behind, and dressed in curls, garlanded with a band of white sarcenet and pale pink roses. A pair of elbow-length gloves, a fan of silk and mother-of-pearl, and a reticule on silken strings were the final accessories chosen to show off her dress, complementing the beautiful pendant round her neck.

It was getting dark outside, and though she felt quite excited about the turn in events, she also felt more than a little worried. Mrs Bennet had said she could telephone her mother, and at the very least, that was what she must do next. Lizzy could not find a single light switch, and resorted to picking up the only candlestick, whose candle was rather badly illuminating the room, as the light was fading. It really did make the place feel very authentic, but never before had she appreciated electricity so much. It was easy to see how the writers of the past were so inspired to write gothic tales of ghostly happenings and ghoulish goings-on. She thought how much more her senses seemed alerted in the dark with only the flickering flame lighting her way. Tiptoeing down the creaking wooden staircase, she frightened herself rather badly once or twice as her own shadow loomed and shrank against the walls like a cowering thief in the night, waiting to pounce.

She found the telephone in the hallway, an object she hadn't noticed being there before and quite incongruous in this setting, which in every other respect made her feel as if she'd travelled back in time. An antique item that looked like a model from the 1930s, Lizzy didn't feel very hopeful on picking up the receiver as all she could hear at the other end were crackling and clicking noises, certainly not like any telephone tone she'd ever heard at home. Inserting her index finger, she set about dialling the number, each turn of the black and white numbered dial swiftly whirring back into place. Then she waited to hear the ringing tone but heard nothing, not a sound, so she tried again thinking she must have dialled incorrectly. It was no use; the line was completely and utterly dead. Still, perhaps Mrs Bennet might know what to do and would help her.

'Are you ready?'

Lizzy recognised the brusque voice that barked out of the darkness and she turned guiltily, as if caught out doing something she shouldn't. He loomed out of the shadows, and for the second time Lizzy actually thought that if Mr Williams didn't look so disapproving he might be considered almost handsome. He was dressed ready to face the cold night air, the cloak he wore made him appear taller than ever and his broad shoulders were just the kind she would admire on anybody else. She really didn't want to ask him to help her, but if she didn't telephone her mother soon, there wouldn't be another opportunity.

'I can't seem to get the telephone to work ... just wondering if it's me.'

Mr Williams picked up the receiver and Lizzy saw him shake his head. 'Nope, it's not working ... completely dead, in fact.'

'Is there another? Or have you a mobile I could use? I really need to phone my mum, and mine's run out of battery.'

'No, that's the only one, and I don't use modern technology, I'm afraid.'

'What about the others? Will anyone else have one?'

'Absolutely not. Look, there's nothing to be done, and if we're not careful we'll be late. It's time to go.'

Lizzy really didn't want to be left on her own with Mr Williams any longer, or have to travel with him by herself. 'Oughtn't we to wait for Mrs Bennet?' she said, thinking that couldn't possibly be the real name of the lady who'd arranged everything.

'No need for that', he said, 'she's left already with her daughters. I'm to escort you, so hurry up before the coachman leaves. He must be thinking we've forgotten him. Here, you'll need this.'

To her great astonishment he took a pink velvet cloak from the coat hooks and held it out so she had no choice but to allow him to place it round her shoulders. She turned and felt the warm silk of the lining envelop her and when she moved back to thank him and before she had a chance to register the fact, he was tying the ribbons at her neck. His fingers brushed her throat momentarily, and she started in surprise. It wasn't an unpleasant feeling, but it disturbed her. When he wasn't looking she rubbed at her neck as if to get rid of the feelings, but the sensations lingered, whatever she did to make them go away.

He picked up his gloves, and stepping in front of her to open the door, to her utter amazement stood aside to let her pass first. So he does have *some* manners then, Lizzy thought, walking on ahead. A liveried footman helped her into the awaiting carriage and Mr Williams followed, seating himself opposite her, before pointedly looking out through the window. Knowing the journey was a short one, Lizzy tried to relax, though it was impossible not to feel very awkward in the silence that was as binding as Mr Williams's dark cloak, wrapped in folds about him. She was determined to make him speak to her.

'Do you go to balls very often, Mr Williams?'

There was a hesitation. 'I do.'

His face turned to hers momentarily, and she met his cold stare. His eyes flicked over her with such studied animosity she didn't know where to look. She felt she was being measured up, evaluated, like some poor animal on sale. Unable to meet his eyes, she stared at his mouth, his lips seemingly incapable of any movement, and set in a hard line. His nostrils flared into an expression that sneered, as if an unpleasant smell emanated from her very being. Right then, Lizzy decided she'd never met such an obnoxious and arrogant man, but she was going to make him talk if it killed her.

'So, am I right in thinking that you enjoy dancing?'

'If I can avoid it, I will.'

'Oh, what a pity, since you go to so many balls. I must admit, I love dancing, though I'm not usually dressed up quite like this.'

'I imagine not.'

Lizzy saw him turn to look through the window once again, as he stifled a yawn. He looked so bored, and so cross, that Mr Williams was beginning to make her feel really cranky, and the last thing she needed was to feel like that.

'So if it's not a daft question, why do you go to so many balls if you don't like them?'

'I am invited.'

'And are they all in Hampshire? Do you ever go to the balls I've heard about in Bath? I've read that people go to Regency balls in Italy and other places abroad.'

'I have been to Bath before.'

'Did you like Bath? I've never been though I've heard it's a lovely place to visit.'

'No, I found the company tedious, to say the least, and rather provincial in outlook.'

He's just an awful snob, thought Lizzy. 'What about London? Have you danced there?'

'On occasion.'

Lizzy briefly wondered if he was capable of stringing a sentence of more than three words together, but she'd reached the point where she couldn't be bothered to find out. Well, she'd tried, but she really didn't want to make any more attempts at conversation. It was too much like hard work.

They were trotting down the long driveway at last, she saw with some relief, and as the other carriages turned in the circle before the great door of Chawton House, Lizzy couldn't help feeling just a little excited. She'd never been to a proper ball before, and one in Regency costume was the stuff of her dreams. She'd soon find her new friends, Lizzy thought, although she really must ask if she could use the phone before she did anything else. Through the window was the sort of scene she'd seen in paintings. A country house of majestic proportions under a blanket of snow, dazzled and shimmered with candlelit interiors, and was lit up from the outside with flares and lanterns casting magical beams of radiant light, turning shadows into swathes of velvet blue and violet. Pretty girls, brilliant in angel-white, holding onto the arms of their handsome beaux, stepped down from a succession of carriages, which rolled around the gravel sweep. There was a sense of anticipation as laughter tinkled in the air like the dangling crystals of chandeliers caught in a sudden breeze.

It was snowing again, and as she stepped down onto the icy carriage step, Lizzy slipped, tumbling over her feet. It felt just like "falling down stairs" in a dream, she thought, twitching and jumping just before one fell asleep, and for a moment she wasn't sure where she was or what she was doing. Everything about the world she found herself in seemed fragile, like the glass snowstorms she loved, broken in an instant unless carefully handled. Mr Williams stepped forward and caught her hand, steadying her gently as she found solid ground, but when she looked up to thank him, he merely looked the other way.

Just as soon as Mr Williams escorted her up the steps, he disappeared. Lizzy saw him briefly chatting to a young man at the head of the reception party, before he clasped the gloved hand of a young woman standing next in line, kissing it before he headed off. Lizzy looked round, feeling a little abandoned, but it wasn't long before she spotted Mrs Bennet and her five daughters. Jane and Elizabeth looked more beautiful than she'd ever imagined in white muslin, a pink sash for Jane and blue for Lizzy. Kitty and Lydia wore shades of pale coral and green, and stood whispering and pointing, mostly at a number of young redcoats who ogled back. Mary looked completely out of place and clung to her father, seemingly reluctant to let go of his arm.

'Lizzy! Over here,' Mrs Bennet beckoned with a wave of her fan. 'Well, I must say you've turned out rather well, that gown is most becoming, though perhaps your lace has slipped a little, dear. Let me fix it for you.' Mrs Bennet fussed about her until she was satisfied. 'Come, let me introduce you to the Bingleys.' She didn't wait to see if Lizzy followed and was off at a pace in front, before suddenly stopping and whirling round as if she'd remembered something of great importance. Mrs Bennet's face loomed large, and Lizzy had to bite her lip to keep a straight face as the former looked from one side of the room to the other, with all the shrewd observance of a spy at large.

'It's Mr Bingley's ball, you know,' she started to say in hushed tones, 'he's shown a very marked interest in my Jane at all the other gatherings, and I have high hopes.'

This was followed by a knowing look, which Lizzy interpreted immediately, being firstly, an expert on the book, *Pride and Prejudice*, and secondly, an avid watcher of any adaptation known to Janeites. Lizzy also felt she was being given fair warning, that Mrs Bennet was letting her know Mr Bingley was "off-limits".

'Do you expect an engagement soon, Mrs Bennet?' asked Lizzy, knowing these were exactly her companion's thoughts.

'I do, indeed,' said Mrs Bennet, nodding furiously and agitating the carefully coiffured curls on her head so much they quivered like a diamond brooch *en tremblant*. 'Tonight may be the occasion when Bingley declares himself - I do hope so. This ball is being given in Jane's honour ... just look, he is besotted!'

They'd reached the reception party, Mrs Bennet pulling her through the awaiting crowd of people to the front. Lizzy saw Jane and Mr Bingley deep in conversation. They only seemed to have eyes for the other, which was lovely to see, but then Lizzy remembered that after the ball Mr Bingley gave at Netherfield in *Pride and Prejudice*, he left next morning without giving Jane any idea of his return. Was that about to happen again? So many things seemed similar to the events in the book, but she didn't know if she could bear to witness what might be Jane's last happy evening.

Mr Bingley introduced his sisters, Miss Caroline Bingley and Mrs Hurst, two very proud young women, to Lizzy's mind, before they were all swept through into the ballroom. Lydia and Kitty were over-excited already, but when they saw Mr Wickham there was no stopping them.

'Oh, he's *here*, Kitty,' Lydia screamed too loudly, so that a party of people standing to her right turned to stare. '*I* must dance with him first, and I've *every* chance of that now our sister has to dance with Mr Collins!'

Both girls laughed uproariously, and Lizzy saw Elizabeth stand stock-still, as she realised Mr Wickham was in the room. She was blushing, and it seemed she was trying her hardest not to draw his attention, but then Lydia rushed over to him and, within seconds, pointed her sister out to him before she laughed again.

Elizabeth ignored them and introduced Lizzy to her friend Charlotte Lucas, whereupon there was an outpouring of all the grievances about Mr Collins she'd been saving up for a week.

'Just look at him, Charlotte. I believe he had the maids dress his hair in rags last night to achieve those curls. Did you ever see such an oddity?'

'But, we should not judge only on appearance, Elizabeth,' said Charlotte, 'and he surely has height in his favour.'

'Without doubt, he's tall enough, which adds a certain pomposity to his manner, but he is overly formal and so grave, that I find I'm inclined to giggle like my youngest sisters every time he opens his mouth. He stated, most seriously, that he has come here to admire us, and at every possible moment he leers and expresses his esteem for the most inane comments uttered by me or my sisters, not to mention his constant fawning over every stick of furniture or piece of silver he imagines comes with the estate.'

'Well, he will inherit, and there is nothing that can be done about that. It may be he is looking for a wife, Eliza, and then all will be safe.'

'Charlotte, I know what that look means. One of my sisters may have him, but you know I could not marry a man I do not love.'

Before much longer, they were joined by Mr Collins, the man himself, who clung, limpet-like, to Elizabeth's side, bowing and offering compliments, talking far too much, completely unaware that his dancing partner for the first dance of the evening was utterly distracted.

Well, this wasn't quite turning out like the Netherfield ball, after all, Lizzy thought. Mr Wickham was there, and she remembered that he'd kept his distance in Jane Austen's novel. It probably wasn't a good idea to think too much about the book she knew so well, but it was confusing. If this was some sort of *Pride and Prejudice* inspired event, they were all performing very well, even if they had the details and the plot all wrong.

She was just watching Mr Collins escort Elizabeth to the dance floor when Mr Williams presented himself, and asked her to dance. Lizzy was so surprised, she agreed before she could think of a single reason to refuse him, and could only hope she wouldn't disgrace herself. Of course, she'd practised Regency dancing many times in front of the television trying to perfect all the dances, but she'd never been to a ball before or stood opposite a partner. It didn't help that Mr Williams looked so cross, and she wondered why he'd asked her. Caroline Bingley, with her proud ways, was surely more his dish of tea.

For the first few moments Lizzy could not think what to say. Besides the fact she had to really concentrate on the steps needed for the dance, she dismissed the idea of any discussion on the subject of dancing after her attempt in the coach. Perhaps she should try being a bit more personal, he seemed just like the kind of guy who would enjoy talking about himself.

'How long have you been at Jane Austen's House?' Lizzy asked.

Silence reigned and Lizzy wondered if he was going to reply at all. 'Oh, that's a difficult question.'

Good Lord, Lizzy thought, was it really that hard? She watched his expression, which was very comical as he raised his eyes, clearly calculating something in his head.

'Well, I suppose it must be getting on for fifteen years or so, though perhaps only for a year, in an official capacity.'

Lizzy frowned. He didn't look much older than about twenty-five or six, and surely it was illegal to employ people under the age of ten or eleven. What could he mean? 'You were a volunteer, perhaps?'

'No, never been in the army, though I know a few who have.'

They separated at this point, to twirl round with other partners, for which Lizzy felt some relief. She half wondered if she was speaking a different language because Mr Williams had no idea what she was talking about. But, she was a sweet girl at heart, and decided to give him one last try.

'So, do you work in a curatorial capacity?'

'My dear, I am a gentleman, I've never worked a day in my life.'

'I'm sorry, I didn't mean to offend you, it's just that you seemed to be shutting up the house when I arrived, and I thought ...'

His face remained implacable. 'Ah, I understand. My role is certainly an unusual one - Miss Austen herself devised it, but has yet to completely decide certain matters pertaining to my position.'

'Oh, I see,' she said, even though she had no idea what he meant.

The dance seemed to last forever and Mr Williams made no attempt at any further conversation. When it was over he simply bowed and walked away. Lizzy had to admit he danced really well, though she'd never give him the satisfaction of telling him.

Elizabeth was standing nearby as she came off the floor and walked over to join her. 'You have met Mr Williams, I see.'

Lizzy observed the twinkle in Eliza's eye, and knew she could be frank. 'What is the matter with him? Tell me, is it possible I am unintelligible?'

'Do not worry, Miss Benson, he is like that with everyone. A prouder, more disagreeable man I have not met. He insists on coming to every event, and then stands around not dancing. I suppose you should feel honoured in one way that he chose to dance with you. However, if I were you, I should not ... I daresay *I* would have refused him.'

'I would have done, Miss Bennet, but he took me by surprise, and before I knew what I'd done I said yes.'

'Well, never mind, I know what will cheer you up. You must come and meet Miss Austen, for if not for her neither you nor I would be here!'

Lizzy couldn't believe her ears, and felt so nervous at the thought of meeting the author of her favourite books in the whole world, she immediately became very flustered. Her mouth dried up, and for a single moment, she couldn't remember any of the names of the books she loved so well.

Leading her to the other end of the ballroom, Miss Bennet took her by the hand to the great fireplace where an enormous log burned in the grate. A small table like the one she'd seen back at the house, with a writing desk on top, was set to one side next to an accompanying chair, but there was no one sitting there. On the table were a bottle of ink, a quill pen and a sheaf of paper much like the ones Lizzy had seen before.

'Oh dear, we appear to have missed her,' said Elizabeth. 'She's very fond of ices - perhaps she'll be found at the refreshment table.'

Lizzy felt very disappointed, and looked about, though how she might recognise Miss Austen, she couldn't say. Every image she'd ever seen of her contradicted the other. Would she really know her if she were to come bounding over? Her eye caught sight of a paragraph of writing on the top of the manuscript.

They had not long separated when Miss Bingley came towards her, and with an expression of civil disdain thus accosted her: -

She heard a step behind them and turned to see Miss Bingley standing there with such a haughty expression on her face that Lizzy wondered why she'd decided to stop and engage them in conversation.

'So, Miss Eliza, I hear you are quite delighted with George Wickham! Your sister has been talking to me about him, and asking me a thousand questions.'

'Mr Wickham is a very pleasant young man,' answered Elizabeth. 'I like him very much.'

'He is of excellent character, certainly,' said Miss Bingley, 'and is to inherit a vast estate in Derbyshire. His mother, Lady Elinor Wickham, is very keen for him to marry well, someone who will bring all the usual desirable attributes and alliances, which some ladies have the good fortune to possess.'

'Any mother would wish her son to marry someone who was accomplished and well-connected,' said Elizabeth.

'Yes, but I know Lady Elinor very well, and she would not look kindly on any young woman, desirous of increasing her own fortunes, who attempted to draw him in.'

Lizzy saw Elizabeth turn scarlet, and realised, as did her friend all too clearly, that Miss Bingley was referring to her. She was confused by the conversation. Wickham, now rich and of excellent character? This was not *Pride and Prejudice* as she remembered it.

'I am sure no mother would want her son hunted down for his fortune,

Miss Bingley.'

Satisfied that she'd made her point and that Elizabeth understood her meaning, Miss Bingley continued.

'Miss Bennet, Miss Benson, are you sitting this one out or are we to have the pleasure of witnessing your pleasure in the dance with Mr Collins and Mr Williams once more?'

'I am engaged to dance with Mr Collins again,' Eliza admitted, disguising her lack of enthusiasm for the prospect of having her toes squashed again, by her light tone of voice, 'but we were just looking for Miss Austen,' Eliza replied. 'Have you happened to see her?'

'I believe she was partaking of ices in the tea room,' said Miss Bingley. 'If you're quick you may just catch her. I must make haste also. I believe I hear the musicians striking up again, and I am to dance next with Mr Wickham. He has marked my card for three dances! I beg your pardon. And, pray excuse my interference, it was kindly meant.'

Lizzy and Elizabeth exchanged glances when she'd gone. 'I can see what you're thinking, Miss Benson, and you are quite right.'

'What an insolent girl, if you don't mind my saying so, Miss Bennet. She wants Mr Wickham for herself, that's very plain to see,' said Lizzy.

'Well, I've no doubt; she'll get him in the end. How could I possibly hope to win his heart or that of his mother? I have no dowry, and no expectation of any money.'

'He could not fail to fall in love with you. You are the prettiest girl in the room.'

'You are very kind, Miss Benson, but perhaps I have been fooling myself to think his regard is anything more than the usual shown to a young woman eager to dance and delight in a young man's company.'

'If he does want Miss Bingley, and her wretched fortune, then good luck to him,' said Lizzy. 'He will always think of you with regret. In any case, perhaps there is someone else for you. Someone you haven't met yet.'

Elizabeth laughed. 'Perhaps you are right, Miss Benson, and when Mr Collins has finished embarrassing me on the dance floor, I fully intend to bump into him.'

'Is Mr Darcy here?' Lizzy asked tentatively.

Elizabeth shook her head. 'I do not recall that name. Darcy, did you say? Is he a friend of yours?'

Lizzy smiled. 'Not really, though I must admit he is someone I would like to know better.'

'Well, my friend, I hope he is here for your sake. One of us must find a husband, and with your wit and beauty you have every chance of securing him.'

Something was not quite right, thought Lizzy. No Mr Darcy? Elizabeth had looked completely blank at the mention of his name. Whatever was being re-enacted here, it surely wasn't *Pride and Prejudice*.

Mr Collins sat at Elizabeth's side whenever he could. Thankfully, during the course of the evening Mr Wickham rescued the latter, on more than one occasion. Lizzy wasn't certain this was such a good idea whatever Miss Bingley had to say on his good character. At least, she decided however unsure *she* might be about him, surely dancing with him had to be a better option than being stuck with Mr Collins. She wanted to help Elizabeth if she could and so took it in turns with Charlotte to entertain him. He seemed to have given up on gaining Kitty's approval whose eyes rolled with horror every time he approached her, and as Miss Lucas seemed able to entertain him amply, after a while Lizzy decided to have a wander in search of a telephone. As she crossed the edge of the ballroom, she caught a fleeting glimpse of a tall girl with chestnut hair falling in soft curls round her face. There was something familiar about her and she wondered if it was Miss Austen she'd spotted until glancing once more, she realised it was her own reflection in a tall pier glass. That made her chuckle out loud. How silly of her to confuse her own image with that of the great author.

Lizzy had a very good view of the dancing, and when Elizabeth and Mr Wickham came down together, hand in hand, she decided they made a very gorgeous couple. They were both good-looking - Mr Wickham in his redcoat was extraordinarily handsome with his neat head of thick dark hair, sparkling eyes full of humour, and a generous mouth easily persuaded into smiling. It was evident that Elizabeth could make him laugh at will, and Lizzy saw how happy she was in his company as their eyes told the story of a great attraction as they flickered and caught, dancing to a time honoured tune. Jane and Bingley were in the same dance, they'd been inseparable all evening. Perhaps the story was going to turn out to be a lot more straightforward, Lizzy wondered, and the girls would get the men they liked on first impression.

There seemed to be the same problem with the telephone when Lizzy found one in a small office located off the hallway. It looked even older than the last one she'd used, and was just as broken. On further enquiry she was told that it was undoubtedly the snow that had cut them off from all civilisation and that there were no more means of communication with the outside world. There wasn't much she could do, it was too late to go wandering off on her own, and as the supper bell sounded, she joined the throng headed for the dining room where long tables groaning under plates of cold ham and chicken were waiting to be consumed.

'Yes, Mrs Lucas,' Mrs Bennet was saying to her neighbour, 'you can be sure I shall see both Jane and Elizabeth married before Valentine's day. It is all going off so well, such splendid young men, and so rich! Mary, Kitty, and Lydia will be so advantaged by such matches, and will, no doubt, meet all of Mr Bingley's and Mr Wickham's friends. Five girls married before the year is out, I can see how it will be!'

Lizzy noted Eliza's expression as she heard her mother spouting off, and she didn't look very happy. She wasn't the only one. Someone else was watching Mrs Bennet with an expression of distaste on his face. Mr Williams was studying her intently and sneering, occasionally passing comment to his companion, which made Lizzy sure he was talking about them all. And when supper was over, and singing was talked of, she saw Mary after very little entreaty, preparing to oblige the company, and Lizzy knew Mr Williams would glower even more.

Elizabeth could bear it no longer. Taking Mary to one side, she managed to persuade her to play instead of sing, and so it was that the two sisters took their places at the piano. Eliza had a sweet singing voice and soon drew an audience around her. Mr Wickham looked on proudly, Miss Bingley and her sister, Mrs Hurst, grudgingly passed their compliments, and Mr Williams, standing closely to the instrument was witnessed watching intently though he kept his thoughts to himself.

It had been a long evening, and when at last they arose to take their leave after dancing every dance, Mrs Bennet pressed both Mr Bingley and Mr Wickham to visit them soon at Chawton cottage, assuring them how happy they would make them by eating a family dinner at any time. Mr Wickham agreed, and Bingley readily accepted, declaring he would be delighted to visit the Bennet family after his return from London, where he was obliged to go the next day for a short time. Alarm bells rang for Lizzy, but she felt she couldn't say a word to Jane. For all she knew, he might be back in a week or two and she would have made her anxious for nothing.

Lizzy was very pleased not to have to travel back to the cottage with Mr Williams, and managed to squeeze in the carriage with the Bennet family. The housekeeper, Mrs Hill, was waiting for them at home, and handed Lizzy a candle to light her way upstairs. Hearing the chattering and laughter of Lydia and Kitty behind her as she turned on the twisting staircase, reminded her how much she missed her sister. They didn't always get on these days but Lily was going through some challenging times as a teenager. It would have been wonderful to be able to share secrets, hopes and dreams with Lily, she thought, as Lydia was regaling her sister about her dance partners. All she could hope was that one day they'd be as close as they once were.

Her bedchamber looked very cosy with the covers on her bed pulled invitingly back. She couldn't believe she was going to sleep in Jane Austen's bed again, and wished, not for the first time, that she could have met the author at the ball. Lizzy supposed she'd just been too busy, probably thinking about what was going to happen next in her novel. How she would have liked to sit and talk to her. She had so many questions: not least, what had happened to Mr Darcy? It was only then that she remembered, "falling" into the Advent calendar, but it was far too late to be deciding whether or not her experience at the ball had been real or imaginary. With images of Colin Firth and Matthew McFadyen dancing before her eyes, she snuffed out the candle, plumped her head down on the pillow and promptly fell asleep.

Chapter 5

Door Number *Five*

The Advent calendar was the first thing she looked for in the morning when she woke. Leaping out of bed, she crossed the room to the chest of drawers whilst blowing on her fingers, which felt almost too cold to manage anything, least of all open the tiny door that was lit beneath by some strange and mysterious light. But, after the magical experience yesterday, she was eager to see what was behind and she felt excited to discover a picture of a letter behind the door of number five. It looked like the folded Georgian ones she'd once seen in a museum display, and she could just make out that the tiny writing had the direction for Chawton Cottage beautifully inscribed in an old-fashioned script, and her name written along the top!

A knock at the door heralded the housemaid, Sally, who entered with a cheerful smile, and an unexpected present.

'Mrs Bennet thought you might need a fresh gown, Miss Benson,' she said. 'You're the same size as Miss Elizabeth, and she thought you might like this one.'

'Oh, that's very kind,' answered Lizzy, 'but I shall be going home today.'

'Very well,' continued Sally, opening the closet, 'though I heard Mrs Bennet say she'd had a letter from your mother with a message that you could stay as long as you like.'

Lizzy was very puzzled, to say the least. 'Goodness, how can that have happened? I didn't think she knew I was here.'

'I can't say, miss, but I'll hang up your gown, and then you can decide. Besides, I do not think you'll be able to go anywhere today. There's been a fresh fall of snow, and it's still falling, as if cook is plucking geese up in the heavens. And, it's so cold out there, you'll turn blue if you're out in it for any length of time. Mrs Hill has the washing dripping all over the kitchen because it turned frozen and stiff like boards outside in the yard.'

Lizzy looked out of the window again to see the sky dark as a pigeon's breast, and swirling snowflakes spinning to the ground. Icicles hung from the roof in a row of diamond needles, and the lane outside showed no visible evidence of last night's carriage wheels, the snow was so high.

Dressing quickly, Lizzy was eager to find out more about the mysterious letter. The gown she pulled on over her head was a pretty striped cotton with classical medallions dotted in between, and fitted her so beautifully that she delighted in examining her reflection in the looking glass before hunger overtook every other thought. The smell of toast and other delicious breakfast aromas were floating upstairs so she hurried down and made her way to the dining parlour. Everyone was seated, except for one space where a blue and white willow patterned plate told her that someone had already eaten and left.

Mrs Bennet saw her staring. 'Mr Williams has left for London though I said he was foolish to think of riding all that way in this dreadful weather. He would insist, and I can only hope he will not regret being so foolhardy.'

Lizzy felt almost sorry that she wouldn't have another opportunity of teasing him. 'Sally said you'd had a letter from my mother.'

'Oh yes, my dear. She said you are not to worry your head about getting home. I have it here somewhere. Although it is addressed to you, I assumed it was for me when I opened it, having mislaid my spectacles.'

A likely story, thought Lizzy. 'But, how did she know I was here?'

'Mr Williams wrote to her the day before yesterday, I believe. He knew the telephone wasn't working and took a chance on the post.'

'Oh, I see, that was very kind of him.' Frankly, she was surprised that he could be so thoughtful, and felt very slightly disappointed that she could not thank him. She was more than a little puzzled at the suggestion that he'd written the day *before* yesterday, but she was beginning to learn that not very much about time in this place made any sense at all.

When she had the letter in her hand, Lizzy had no doubt it was from her mother. It certainly was her handwriting, and from its tone, it simply couldn't be from anyone else.

Dear Lizzy,

I hope you're well and having a lovely time at Chawton cottage. Mr Williams wrote to tell me about the severe weather in Hampshire, which is now completely spread nationwide. Apparently, it's the worst snow since 1811 - fancy that! Mr Williams sounds a nice young man, and when I googled him, I must admit I was very impressed. Apparently, he's related to an earl in Derbyshire, did you know that? He's very handsome, isn't he? Please don't worry about trying to get home just yet. Have fun, and we'll see you when the snow stops - though, even then don't worry if you're having a good time. Mr Williams said he was going to try and get to London before the weather really turned for the worse, but that he was also trying to get home for Christmas. What a pity there is little chance of you being able to travel to Derbyshire because I'm sure if you and he spent any time together, you'd get on like a house on fire. Still, I am glad you are making some new friends, especially after you had your heart broken by your so-called 'best friend's' brother. I'm not one to bear grudges but if I ever see that two-timing layabout in Barnet High Street again, I shall give him a piece of my mind. Well, I won't say any more on that subject, but a good-looking young man with plenty of money might be the best way to heal your pain.

Your loving Mum.

xxx

Lizzy was mildly amused by her mother's letter. Though she always had her best interests at heart, her mum tirelessly worked to find as many opportunities as she could for Lizzy to meet new friends, especially those she considered suitable young men. It was a bit like being in *Pride and Prejudice*, she thought; as her mother was as keen as Mrs Bennet to help her find the "right young man". Well, she could think again when it came to Mr Williams. She didn't care who his father was or where he lived in Derbyshire, and she could only hope she'd be on her way home before much longer.

Mr Collins was just finishing his breakfast, and was dabbing at his mouth with a napkin when he coughed, rather loudly, to gain Mrs Bennet's attention. 'May I hope, madam, for the honour of a private audience with your fair daughter in the course of this morning?'

Elizabeth blushed with surprise, but Mrs Bennet instantly answered, 'Oh dear! Yes - certainly. I am sure Eliza will be very happy - I am sure she can have no objection. Come, girls … Jane, Mary, Kitty and Lydia … now, I want you up stairs.'

'Dear ma'am, I beg you will not go,' Elizabeth cried out as she saw her mother about to rush off. 'Mr Collins must excuse me. He can have nothing to say to me that anybody need not hear.'

'Nonsense, Elizabeth,' Mrs Bennet retorted. 'I desire you will stay where you are … indeed, Eliza, I *insist* upon your staying and hearing Mr Collins.'

Lizzy had an idea what was coming and it was obvious that Elizabeth had too by the frightened expression on her face. Lizzy only managed a bite of toast and butter before Mrs Bennet was shooing them all out of the room. They stood in the vestibule, nudging and whispering to one another, none of them making any attempt to go upstairs. Mrs Bennet was the worst of them all, standing with her ear to the door.

Whilst they were standing there a sudden loud knocking at the front door had Mrs Hill bustling along the passageway to see who was calling, and adding to the general sense of commotion.

Mr Wickham bowed, and entered. Mrs Bennet, on seeing the gentleman blushed scarlet. She still openly admired a redcoat and Mr Wickham made such a handsome picture.

'Good morning, Mrs Bennet,' he said with a deep bow. 'I hope you are well.'

Having assured him she was quite well, she was now looking a little distracted, having her attention equally divided between what was going on beyond the parlour door and wondering why Mr Wickham had called.

'I wondered, ma'am, if I might prevail upon you to request an audience with your daughter Elizabeth?'

Mrs Bennet's brain was soon working overtime. Wickham was a much better bet than Mr Collins even if the latter were to inherit the house. And if she was clever about it, she might be able to convince him to court one of the others. But what could she do? It might already be too late!

She turned to her eldest daughter. 'Jane, my dear, please tell Eliza I wish to speak to her immediately. Quickly, dear - make haste. RUN, Jane ... run!'

Knowing her sister must be suffering all kinds of mortification at the hands of Mr Collins, Jane immediately dashed to Elizabeth's rescue. Mr Collins looked most displeased at being interrupted, but Eliza was so relieved that she hugged her sister as she left the room. Hurrying behind her, the young rector spoke in an endless stream of verbose flattery, still giving his reasons for his proposal, his voice growing ever louder.

'And now nothing remains for me but to assure you in the most animated language of the violence of my affection. I declare I am in love with you, Miss Bennet!'

Still pronouncing his intentions, Mrs Bennet cut him off mid-flow before he could continue. Taking his arm, and reversing his direction she proceeded to escort him into the drawing room.

'Mr Collins, have I shown you the view from the drawing room window? It is a fine one overlooking the gardens.'

'Mrs Bennet,' he replied, trying to extricate himself from her firm hold on his person, 'perhaps I did not make my feelings or intentions clear. I was in the midst of a proposal, an offer of marriage to Miss Elizabeth before Miss Bennet's untimely interruption and, moreover, if it was not plain before then allow me now to express it - my whole reason for coming into Hertfordshire was with the design of selecting a wife, as I certainly have, singling out Elizabeth as the companion of my future life! But, perhaps it will be advisable for me to state that I wish to conclude my conference with Elizabeth - immediately. She has not yet heard all my reasons for marrying.'

'Ah yes, Mr Collins, I understand,' said Mrs Bennet patting his arm reassuringly. 'Perhaps I did not fully comprehend your interests in proposing marriage to Elizabeth or I should certainly have prevented Mr Wickham from seeing her. I'm afraid you may have been thwarted in regard to an alliance as I have high expectations that Elizabeth is accepting Mr Wickham's offer at this moment. Notwithstanding this fact, I know of no attachments amongst my younger daughters. Mary is a sensible girl, sir, I think you will find she would make you an ideal bride.'

'Mary? Let me see, which one is she?'

'My middle daughter, Mr Collins, and I might add a most suitable candidate for a clergyman's wife. Why, she has Fordyce's Sermons almost off pat!'

'Ah, the plain girl - I am not certain if Miss Mary and I would suit, though I am sure she is an excellent creature.'

'Her looks may not be her foremost attraction, sir, but she is of sound mind. A lady's wits may keep one amused long after her looks have gone, and I'm sure there are none so well-versed in Bible tracts and moral underpinning as my Mary.'

'An attractive proposition, Mrs Bennet, but nevertheless ...'

'Now Kitty, I think you will agree, has looks to charm and a very fine figure, even if she is on the short side. And if her teeth are not quite so straight as dear Jane's or her hair not quite as curly as Elizabeth's, I think she presents well on the whole. She is just coming out this season, and so no suitors are yet calling.'

'She laughs too much.'

'Not nearly so much as she should for such a young person, Mr Collins. Kitty is a sweet ripe cherry, sir, just waiting to be plucked for matrimony, and a little harmless laughter just shows how very biddable she can be. To be always in good humour is an asset for any clergyman's wife.'

'Perhaps you have a point, Mrs Bennet. A young girl can be easily trained, I think.'

'Oh, certainly, sir - trained to do your bidding, I can assure you.'

Just at that moment, Elizabeth opened the door. Talking in an animated fashion with Mr Wickham hanging on her every word, she escorted him to the front door where she waved him goodbye.

Mrs Bennet could wait no longer and marching over to her daughter whispered loudly in her ear. 'Well, Eliza, when are we to expect your wedding?'

Lizzy answered with no modulation, not caring if Mr Collins heard every word, though she saw him head off to the sitting room in search of other company. 'I am sure Mr Collins knows I desire no such thing, Mama. He tried to propose, but very fortunately Mr Wickham came to call in my hour of need.'

'I am not talking of Mr Collins,' said her mother with great exasperation. 'When are you to marry Mr Wickham?'

Elizabeth laughed. 'Mr Wickham did not come to propose, Mama! Whatever can have given you such an idea? He came to tell me his regiment is called to Derbyshire. He is pleased to be returning for his family seat, Holmeshaw Hall, is in the county.'

'He is leaving? And when is he coming back?'

'I know of no plans for his return, Mama.'

'In that case, you can marry cousin Collins. Run after him and tell him you'd like to hear what he has to say, that you were rudely interrupted this morning, and you are more than willing to accept any proposal.'

'But that would not be telling the truth, Mama, and in any case, I see him talking to Kitty in the sitting room. I would hate to interrupt them, though judging from my sister's expression, an intervention could not come too soon.'

Chapter 6

Door Number *Six*

After breakfast the next morning, there was a plan to walk to Alton. The snow was stopping and it was one of those crisp, sunny days where the blue sky reminded one of summer until you stepped outside and felt the cold. Lizzy had begun to feel at home in Chawton cottage, and though she wondered for a moment whether she should attempt to try and get home, she decided she really would like to stay a little longer. Elizabeth and Jane were both friendly and charming, she thought of them almost like the sisters she'd never had. Her own sister Lily was a bit of a handful, to put it mildly. Lizzy supposed it had a lot to do with her age being just sixteen, but Lily didn't appear to think of anything else but boys, and all her friends were the same. Lily wasn't a bit like Lizzy who liked to spend her free time reading and enjoying time spent at home. So to be spending her days with girls who shared similar interests and who enjoyed intelligent conversation was a complete change. Not that they were serious all the time. Being privy to some of their private conversations had shown her what fun they were to be around. Jane was a little more sensitive, but Lizzy's witty remarks made her smile again and again.

As soon as they were ready, the girls set off, a picture in vermilion cloaks making a bright foil against the snow and pine trees like holly berries amongst glossy leaves. Everyone was talking excitedly, nineteen to the dozen, discussing Christmas celebrations and presents they were thinking of buying or making.

'I'm making Captain Denny a handkerchief,' Lizzy overheard Lydia whisper rather loudly to her sister Kitty. 'Mrs Hill let me have a strip of cambric, and she's showing me how to embroider the initials.'

'For goodness' sake, don't let Eliza or Jane hear you or it will be confiscated in a moment,' her sister replied.

'Yes, they're already saying I talk too much to him, but he is so handsome in his red coat, I cannot resist him!'

'He is handsome, though I'm very struck on Captain Long. He has the bluest eyes I ever saw.'

'I shall insist Captain Denny keeps his kerchief next to his heart,' said Lydia, ignoring Kitty, a dreamy expression coming over her countenance. 'I shall sprinkle a little of my scent on it so he always thinks of me.'

'I must admit I am all astonishment at your sudden industry - when did you become such a keen needlewoman?'

'Oh, Kitty, I have no intention of sewing it myself. Mrs Hill will soon see I have no aptitude - I can always get round her, and she will do it for me!'

They were incorrigible, Lizzy thought, but didn't really think they were very much different from her sister and some of the friends she'd known as she was growing up. Lydia and Kitty were clearly equally as boy-mad, and even she could see the attraction of a man in uniform.

As they walked along she looked out for recognisable landmarks. Alton High Street had a look of the familiar in some of the older buildings, but Lizzy knew immediately something was not quite right. There wasn't a car in sight; only gigs and carriages, horses and carts were to be seen along the length of the road. Not a single sign of modern life existed; every plastic shop front, lampposts, telephone boxes, and people dressed as she expected, were gone. It simply wasn't possible for the whole town to be in on the *Pride and Prejudice* play, she thought, as she saw the numbers of people dressed in Regency clothes going about their business. It was all so strange. Had she time travelled, she wondered? Yet, it wasn't possible to go back in time in someone else's book, Lizzy reasoned, though she had an idea that perhaps the Advent calendar and Jane Austen's house were at the root of it. Perhaps Chawton cottage was enchanted, under a magical spell, and that idea she could more easily believe. Jane Austen's books always felt like entering a special kind of fairyland - they transported her to other worlds where she never wanted to leave. Well, it was either that or someone had knocked her on the head, she was lying in a coma and having drug-induced nightmares - she wasn't sure which.

Lydia and Kitty made for the nearest milliner's shop, declaring they had no intention of buying one, but were determined on trying every one if Miss Allsop, the milliner, would oblige them. Lizzy followed Jane, Elizabeth and Mary into the bookshop where they spent some time choosing a new volume of poems for their father.

'I think Papa might enjoy some Wordsworth,' said Jane.

'He is not very romantic,' said Elizabeth, 'but I agree, he might like to abuse them and always loves to add to his collection. If we put together we can buy both volumes. I would love to visit Wordsworth country, myself.'

'Doesn't Mr Wickham come from that part of the country?' Jane asked.

'No, not so far north, but Derbyshire, I hear, is also beautiful.'

'And rendered more so with the handsome Mr Wickham in situ,' added Jane with a laugh. 'Oh, if only young men did not have to go so far away on business.'

'Oh, Jane, I know Mr Bingley will soon be back again. London will hold no charms for him.'

'And let us hope Mr Wickham's regiment find themselves pining for the plains of Hampshire!'

Mr Denny walked in then with Captain Long, followed in hot pursuit by Lydia and Kitty.

Captain Denny bowed. 'Good morning, ladies. How lovely it is to see all the Miss Bennets in town on such a chilly day. It warms the cockles of our hearts, does it not, Captain Long?'

'Good morning, Captain Denny and Captain Long,' Jane answered. 'Are you shopping for Christmas presents?'

'No, Miss Bennet, we're on our way to see Colonel Forster for a military drill. It won't be quite the same now our number is halved ... some of our fellow soldiers have moved on, y'know.'

'Yes, Mr Wickham told me himself that he was going to Derbyshire,' answered Eliza.

'We miss his society most particularly, Miss Elizabeth. There never was a finer fellow, as cheerful as you are ever likely to meet, but full of regret to be leaving, I know.'

Lizzy saw her friend blush before Lydia spoke up.

'Will they be staying there for long, Captain Denny?' she asked. 'Elizabeth would like to know when Mr Wickham is to return.'

'I believe he is to spend some time in Derbyshire, but I am unable to tell you more.'

'I hope you're not going away, Captain Denny,' Lydia continued, looking up at him from under her fluttering lashes.

'As a matter of fact we shall be travelling to join Mr Wickham's regiment on exercises very soon. The county offers a different terrain and will make an excellent training ground.'

'Oh no! What shall we do for society when you are all gone? How we shall miss you!' she declared, until a warning glance or two from her sisters silenced her momentarily.

Shortly afterwards, they separated from the soldiers with promises to meet at the next evening party. The girls' shopping took up a pleasant morning, and several presents were found. A bottle of lavender water was chosen for Mrs Bennet, a new comb for their Aunt Gardiner's hair, a bodkin for Aunt Phillips, and new ribbons for their own Christmas gowns were chosen. It was a happy walk home trudging through the snow, and even Mary seemed in good spirits.

But, their happiness was short-lived. The early afternoon brought some very sad news for Jane. Lizzy hadn't meant to eavesdrop but she heard the sisters discussing a letter that had arrived from Caroline Bingley that very morning. It stated that the Bingleys visit to London would not be so swiftly over, and that they would be staying there for the winter. Jane was clearly very upset, as Miss Bingley had hinted that she would be glad her brother would be enjoying a wider society. It had always been his father's preference that he should continue to raise the family name and fortunes with an alliance from one of the very best families, she wrote, and that in London, he could be in no better position. Her letter assured Jane that her friendship was the only thing Miss Bingley was sorry to leave behind.

Elizabeth made her feelings on the subject very clear. 'Miss Bingley knows her brother is in love with you, and so she is keeping him away. Miss Bingley is clawing her way up society's ladder and is on the lookout for a titled lady for him, you mark my words. She knows if Charles Bingley stays in Chawton he will marry you in the spring and she will not have any control over him or his household any longer.'

'Elizabeth, there is more: *I sincerely hope your Christmas in Hampshire may abound in the gaieties which that season generally brings, and that your beaux will be so numerous as to prevent your feeling the loss of our company.*' Jane looked up from the letter and Lizzy could see how very upset she was feeling. '*Clearly, Miss Bingley has no idea how I feel about her brother or she could not have written such a letter.*'

'And no one could doubt his affection for you either. Do not trust Miss Bingley, she is no true friend, believe me, I know I am right.'

'I would not like to think ill of her.'

'Jane, think as you choose, but in any case, I believe your handsome Mr Bingley will return. He will not be able to stay away, you'll see.'

Miss Bennet seemed cheered by her sister's words. Not one to dwell on unhappiness she changed the conversation to the subject of the dinner that day, which they were to attend at the Lucas's.

When Lizzy went to change for dinner later that afternoon she remembered the calendar. Number six was lighted up, as usual, and when she opened it she found a picture of two painted birds sitting on a branch of pink blossoms behind its door. Two doves with their necks entwined looked a sweet picture of affection, and when they took flight and swooped around her chamber, Lizzy was utterly enchanted. They held a blue ribbon in their beaks, which formed a heart in loops and swirls as they flew up to the rafters and back again. The birds were a heavenly shade of pale grey, unlike any she'd ever seen, and they circled the room before settling back, cooing and preening, through the doorway from which they'd come.

So far, every picture had proved to represent something she had seen during the course of the day, but a pair of lovebirds? Unless the reference somehow implicated Mr and Mrs Bennet, and she thought that highly unlikely, Lizzy couldn't think what it could possibly mean.

Dinner with the Lucas's was a rather quiet affair. Mrs Bennet who had now been told that the Bingleys were not coming back as quickly as she hoped tried to deflect Lady Lucas's questions on the subject.

'Did you hear, Mrs Bennet, it's likely the Bingleys will remain in town all winter,' said Lady Lucas, hardly able to keep the glee out of her voice.

'I know nothing of such tittle-tattle, Lady Lucas. I'm sure Mr Bingley is his own master and will come back to Netherfield just as soon as he pleases.'

'But, I have it on good authority from Jones, the butcher in Lambton. He says all orders are cancelled until further notice as Miss Bingley insisted they would be in London for the whole season.'

'I would not trust the word of butcher Jones, Lady Lucas. I daresay Miss Bingley's preference for Mr Green's meat in Alton is behind *his* disgruntled remarks.'

'Well, it will be a very bad thing for Miss Bennet if what he says is true,' Lady Lucas added, though she had the courtesy to lower her voice so only Mrs Bennet could hear her. 'We all thought they'd be engaged by Christmas, and what with Miss Elizabeth turning down Mr Collins as well, you must be feeling very aggrieved, my dear.'

'I am sure Mr Bingley will return, dear friend, though it will, undoubtedly, be very hard on my poor Jane if she has to wait until after Christmas. As for Mr Collins, I have high hopes there may well be a match with Kitty. He does seem to show her a marked attention.'

The ladies looked across the table where they could both see him giving his full consideration to someone else entirely. Miss Charlotte Lucas was chatting merrily away, and Kitty who was talking to the eldest Lucas boy looked most unconcerned.

Elizabeth could not help remarking on the fact that Miss Lucas was doing more than her fair share of entertaining their cousin. 'She is a friend of all friends, Lizzy, and how I shall ever repay her I do not know. And she is so convincing, to look at her countenance one might almost think she was enjoying herself.'

'Your mother seems reconciled, Miss Bennet,' said Lizzy.

'I am certain she has not yet forgiven me, no matter how appearances look, but after all, she steered Mr Collins away at the crucial moment. I could hardly run and beg him to marry me after she made it perfectly clear that Mr Wickham was her preference.'

'So would you have accepted Mr Collins if he'd been able to finish his declaration?' Lizzy asked.

'Of course not, dear Miss Lizzy, and my mother is fully aware that in such an endeavour she could never succeed, however she protests to the contrary.'

Lizzy felt pleased that however mixed up events appeared to be, at least there was one outcome that was not altered too significantly, and she felt relieved for Elizabeth that she would still not be entering matrimony with cousin Collins!

Chapter 7

Door Number *Seven*

The following morning Lizzy woke early, and found she could not go back to sleep. Sally brought in her steaming water with a clean napkin so she decided to delay no longer but get washed and dressed whilst the water was hot and before ice formed and tinkled in the large lustre jug. Choosing a printed muslin from the closet, she then arranged her hair as she liked. It seemed to take no time at all, her fingers now being accustomed to twisting her locks into a bun on top of her head. She secured the knot with a tortoiseshell comb and decided she was ready to face the day. The house was quiet except for the sounds of servants' footsteps going about their daily tasks, making the wooden stairs creak. Outside beyond the casement, the sounds of horses in the yard and the cows being herded after milking were becoming a familiar part of her day; the farmhands coaxing the doe-eyed creatures gently as they led them back to the fields.

She'd been told that Miss Austen was still staying up at the Great House, but Lizzy wondered if she missed her own bed or the freedom to do as she wished. Eliza said that Jane much preferred being at home where she could be herself, and where she needn't talk to people unless she wished it. Above all, she was able to write at leisure in the cottage, and she was working on a big project, a secret from all but her sister Cassandra.

When Lizzy walked into the dining parlour she could find no sign of anyone else being up, except on closer inspection she saw that Miss Austen's writing table had new papers upon it, a newly sharpened quill, and a fresh pot of ink. There were also a teabowl and a small plate, upon which the evidence of crumbs gave rise to the speculation that perhaps the owner of the items had broken her fast. Could she be back? Once again, Lizzy saw the top of the page, the blots, the crossings out and holes where the manuscript had been corrected.

Charlotte herself was tolerably composed.

That was all Lizzy could see, and as she stood wondering if she dare nudge the paper to see a little more, a movement through the window caught her eye, and she saw a girl, warmly dressed in a hooded cloak trudging through the snow towards the house. It could only be one person, she thought. Lizzy heard a knock at the door, and the sound of welcoming noises.

'Charlotte, you came! I did not expect to see you today,' she heard Elizabeth say.

The door behind Lizzy opened to admit the two young ladies, clearly very pleased to be in one another's company, and when they saw Lizzy they greeted her as if she were as dear to them as each other.

Not as outwardly attractive as her friend Eliza, Miss Lucas had a homely face, Lizzy thought, and a gentle expression.

'Elizabeth, I have some news to impart, my dear friend,' Charlotte said, before casting a glance in Lizzy's direction.

Miss Lucas seemed tolerably composed, thought Lizzy, guessing what she might have to say next. She would surely want to speak to Elizabeth in private. 'Excuse me, but I think I must go,' said Lizzy. 'I really must not intrude.'

'No, please stay, Miss Benson,' Charlotte urged. 'Indeed, I will feel more able to speak if you are here.'

'Goodness, Charlotte, what on earth can be the matter?' said Eliza. 'You're as white as a sheet.'

'I am very well, but something has happened, such a momentous event that I am still reeling from the shock of it.'

'Well, do not delay, my friend, we are all ears!'

'I could not wait to tell you even though I am not certain what you shall think about any of it. No, that is not true. I have a very good idea what you will think about it, but I hope you will be able to reconcile yourself to the idea of such an attachment.'

'An attachment?' Elizabeth declared unable to keep the excitement from her voice. 'Charlotte, this is news indeed!'

'And one, however uncertain of bringing happiness is more than I could ask given that I have reached the age of twenty seven, and have very little fortune. I beg you do not disapprove, Eliza.'

'Charlotte, this is all so sudden. Do not leave us in suspense any longer.'

'He will be my husband however irksome you might find his company, however disagreeable you have proclaimed his society. Elizabeth, I can delay telling you no longer. I am engaged to Mr Collins.'

Lizzy saw the flush rise on Elizabeth's face, her dark curls trembling with every expression of indignation and surprise.

'Engaged to Mr Collins! My dear, Charlotte, impossible!'

Elizabeth laughed out loud and Lizzy saw Charlotte's face falter momentarily. She bit her lip before raising her eyes to meet those of her friend with a steadiness of purpose.

'Why should you be surprised, my dear Eliza? Do you think it incredible that Mr Collins should be able to procure any woman's good opinion, because he was not so happy as to succeed with you? He is offering a comfortable home and other advantages such as the pleasant society of his patroness, Lady Catherine de Bourgh.'

Elizabeth looked as if she realised she'd been too hasty in giving her opinion so candidly. 'My dear, Charlotte, I am wholly thankful to think of your relationship, to consider that we will be true cousins when you are united by this marriage. Please believe me when I say that I wish you all imaginable happiness.'

'I see what you are feeling,' replied Charlotte; 'you must be surprised, very much surprised, so lately as Mr Collins was wishing to marry you. But when you have had time to think it all over, I hope you will be satisfied with what I have done. I am not romantic, you know; I never was. I ask only a comfortable home; and considering Mr Collins's character, connections, and situation in life, I am convinced that my chance of happiness with him is as fair as most people can boast on entering the marriage state.

'Undoubtedly.'

Lizzy sensed the awkwardness between them, and felt the change in the strained atmosphere, which settled in the room like the cloak of snow smothering the landscape outside.

'Well, I just came to tell you my news,' said Charlotte, speaking after an awkward pause. 'I must go home now, there is always so much to do at this busy time of the year.

'Yes, of course,' Eliza replied, 'I have some work of my own to do.'

The girls rose from their seats and Eliza saw her friend to the door.

Elizabeth Bennet and Charlotte Collins did not see eye to eye on the subject of marriage, Lizzy knew. She could not blame Elizabeth for sounding or looking so shocked. She would never marry for convenience, and was plainly shocked to think her best friend could actually allow herself to wed a man she did not love.

Lizzy made her excuses giving Eliza time to reflect on what had happened. As she made her way upstairs to her chamber she heard an awful commotion in the vestibule, an exchange of words, and raucous laughter that could only belong to Lydia. Charlotte's father, Sir William Lucas, had called to tell them the news. Lydia made a great point of telling him he was quite wrong, that Mr Collins was all set to marry her sister, whereupon Elizabeth offered her congratulations in a most decided manner. Mrs Bennet hardly spoke a word whilst he was there, but the minute he'd gone she gave full vent to her feelings and remonstrated, most vociferously, with her daughter.

Lizzy kept out of the way. Below she could hear Mrs Bennet screeching and protesting whilst Elizabeth merely kept her countenance by refusing to be drawn in to such fruitless exchange. Lizzy was becoming used to Mrs Bennet's moods and seeing how each family member dealt with them. But, even when they were all at odds with one another, Lizzy was relishing every moment she spent in the house. Standing by the window she couldn't help thinking how fond she was growing of the cottage and its surroundings. It was all so different to the London suburb where she lived with its sprawling mass of houses built to accommodate the growing numbers of commuters who were shuffled up and down the underground tracks to work in the city every day. All she could see here were fields and trees, a whitened landscape stretching before her, seemingly, with no end. As she stood and stared she saw Jack, the servant boy, leading the donkey and its cart from the small barn at the back of the house. He patted the donkey's neck, and offered him something from his pocket to munch on. Lizzy heard the back door open and saw a figure cross the yard with a light step. It was a young lady she'd not seen before. Tall and slim, she was wearing a rather worn, brown pelisse, slightly mud-spattered at the hem. It was impossible to see her face as Lizzy only had her back view, plus the girl was wearing a felt bonnet, which didn't help. Rather annoyingly, the donkey cart was turned in the direction of the nearest gate, and so it was going to be impossible to get any closer look at the mysterious person. Lizzy watched her run to the gig and step up onto the boards as if she were used to riding in such a carriage very often, and then within another moment Jack had handed her the reins and was urging the donkey on.

'Back we go my lovely, Viola,' Lizzy heard her say. 'Goodbye, Jack, and thank you - that was so kind of you to respond so quickly to my message and arrange for me to come home, however fleetingly.'

Lizzy had a good idea she knew exactly whom it was driving off in the cart, shaking the reins in one hand whilst simultaneously holding on to her hat with the other - it could be no one else. So Miss Austen had been back to the house briefly, and Lizzy was sure she'd been writing. How she wished she'd been seconds earlier and caught her scribbling away at her desk! Lizzy could only hope that now she'd caught a glimpse of Jane she'd see her again very soon.

She didn't want to go back downstairs just yet; Lizzy could still hear the rumblings and whining complaints of Mrs Bennet resonating through the boards under her feet. The fire in her chamber was lit and she decided to take full advantage of her solitude by sitting in an armchair and reading a book from the shelf. Taking up the volume she began to read, a joyful pastime by a warming fire, which normally would have filled all her senses with pleasure.

Besides having her reading perpetually interrupted by Mrs Bennet's occasional piercing rant, her eyes were also drawn to the Christmas calendar on the dressing table. Number seven was glowing, and she couldn't resist getting up to discover what was behind its door. It was a winter's scene of a landscape, one of high peaks, rocks and mountains. She looked at the beautiful picture; it was a painting in miniature, exquisitely executed with the finest brush strokes she ever saw. On closer inspection, Lizzy thought she saw something moving, but was convinced it was just a trick of the light, at first. And then round a bend on the road, which curved along the valley, two carriages laden down with boxes and luggage, including two Christmas turkeys and three braces of pheasants dangling from its roof, were seen travelling along and away into the distance. Lizzy watched it all with astonishment until they disappeared out of sight. She blinked and the tiny carriages were gone leaving the picture restored to its lifeless state.

There seemed to be a momentary lull downstairs. She could hear several comings and goings, and Lydia pronouncing loudly that it was a good job she walked to Alton so often or they would never receive the post. Lizzy chuckled to herself at the idea of Lydia doing anything to benefit anyone else. They were very lucky to get their post by the afternoon, for it was very likely that Lydia and her sister had been visiting Captain Denny and his friends all morning.

It was very quiet in the house; everyone must be reading their letters, she thought. Of course no one would be sending her any, and she didn't feel she could intrude upon their family time, especially if Mrs Bennet was still feeling cross. Then she heard Mrs Bennet exploding again, but this time exclaiming in a voice that was quite changed from her earlier vexatious one. Lizzy crept out onto the landing to hear more.

'Oh, my dears! What a timely invitation! My dear brother, he cannot possibly know how much his invitation gladdens my heart.'

The parlour door opened. Someone was running upstairs, and Lizzy knew she would be caught in the act of eavesdropping. Thank goodness it was only Eliza who turned the stair at the top and stood before her, a huge grin on her face.

'Oh, thank the Lord! Lizzy, you'll never guess what's happened - my uncle has saved the day. They were to come here for Christmas, but at the last minute their plans have changed, and what is more, so have ours!'

'Your mother sounds much happier,' Lizzy answered with a smile.

'She has done nothing but scold me since Sir William Lucas came to tell her the news. At least we will not have to bear Mr Collins' company any longer if we are to go to Derbyshire.'

'You are going to Derbyshire?'

'My uncle finds he has to look after a property belonging to one of his illustrious clients. The gentleman who owns Darley Manor is a very wealthy gentleman, by all accounts. He winters in Italy, but worries incessantly about his house being ransacked in his absence, despite an army of servants who help to keep the bandits at bay. To cut a long story short, my Uncle Gardiner is to act as guardian, and is allowed to invite whosoever he likes to spend Christmas with his family at Darley Manor!'

'How very exciting - I am sure you will all have a wonderful time. Tell me, how far away from Darley Manor is Holmeshaw Hall?'

'Miss Benson, you have a very wicked gleam in your eye,' admonished Eliza. 'I believe it is but a mile away, not that the nearness of Mr Wickham's abode has anything to do with my present excitement at the scheme. I must admit; my reasons for my delight at such a venture are entirely selfish. My mother needs a great distraction from the whole business that has taken place, and I am thrilled that this invitation is so timely. She will be completely taken up with plans for our departure, and will already be plotting to find out who else of note lives in the area, not to mention being beside herself with the excitement of the prospect of living in a grand house for two or three weeks.'

'I am so very pleased for you,' said Lizzy, 'and though I shall be glad to go home in many respects, I must say I shall miss you very much!'

'Miss me?' exclaimed Miss Bennet. 'You cannot go home now, you will break our hearts - we've all grown so very fond of you. Why, Mama mentioned it just now and wanted me to insist that you accompany us. Are you quite ready for the wildness of Derbyshire, Miss Benson, with its great rocks and mountains?'

Lizzy thought of the picture in the calendar, and knew just how it would be. With a mixture of excitement and fear she acknowledged her great inclination for the scheme and accepted Eliza's kind invitation.

Chapter 8

Door number *Eight*

After that day, time at Chawton cottage, and the calendar, which had seemed to work so magically together, began to alter. When Lizzy woke the next morning and attempted to open the door she found it was stuck and resisted being opened at first. There was no glow of light behind the perforations of door number eight, as there had been previously, and it simply wouldn't open. She didn't want to force it; the calendar was such a beautiful and precious object that she hadn't the heart to tear it. If she thought about what had happened to her over the last week or so, dwelling too much on trying to reason exactly what was going on, she concluded that therein lay the road to madness. The only way she could keep her sanity and make sense of the whole experience was to tell herself that she'd fallen into a parallel universe, one that she'd often dreamt of visiting. She was fairly certain that it wasn't just that she was dreaming - never before had she been able to sustain so much action when sleeping, but trying to analyse it all was getting her nowhere. That magic of some kind, the sort she'd believed in as a child, held some enchantment over the whole episode was an unshaken conviction, and she was glad, that even though she was twenty-one and well past childhood days, that such a powerful spell had charmed her. She resolved to think no more on it, and accept it for what it seemed - an extraordinary Christmas gift. It came as almost no surprise that as soon as she'd accepted this, the little door of number eight flew open of its own accord, and Lizzy saw a magician's hat. At least, she thought it might have been, but on reflection she decided it could just as well belong to a gentleman like Mr Bingley, as there wasn't a rabbit in sight. But, it did look rather special, and the pair of gloves draped next to it brought a certain gentleman into her mind. Not that there was anything remotely magical about Mr Williams, Lizzy thought, with a little chuckle to herself.

The house was in an uproar, and everyone occupied with the business of getting ready to depart for Derbyshire. Sally came to help her pack her trunk after breakfast, and took down the gowns hanging from the closet to fold them carefully. There were six day gowns and two evening dresses, four of which Lizzy had never seen before. When she commented on the fact and wondered where they'd come from, Sally's reply surprised her.

'Well, Miss Benson, they've been here all along ... fancy you not noticing.'

Lizzy did not want to contradict her, though she was absolutely certain she'd never seen three of the day dresses or the other evening gown. She watched Sally pick up the printed gown she'd worn the day before. Turning it inside out, as quick as a flash, she shook it before laying it down carefully on the bed to fold and pack.

'Oh, Miss, now that will be lovely to wear at Christmas,' she said.

Lizzy, who'd turned to pick up her hairbrush and the combs from her dressing table was astonished to see that instead of the rather worn muslin with printed medallions, a gown of the finest white silk with the sheerest gauze overlaid on top was now lying on the bed.

'How did you do that?' Lizzy asked, and saw a secret smile form on Sally's lips.

'Oh, it's nothing, Miss - just a little trick I picked up as an under maid.

Just a short flick, and a gown is so much fresher for it.'

'But, it looks more than just freshened up,' Lizzy exclaimed, 'it's like a brand new dress!'

'I don't know, Miss, I'm sure,' answered Sally, beaming with a huge smile, 'but now you come to mention it, I suppose it does look rather fine. Now, come along, I've finished with the gowns, let us find your fan and reticule, and you'll be wanting your shawl - I've heard it's very cold in Derbyshire.'

Lizzy passed over the items one by one. Slippers, half-boots and dancing shoes were added until there was no more room. She could not believe what she'd just witnessed, though began to doubt her own eyes. Sally was so matter-of-fact about it that she wondered if the dress had been there all along.

'There, we're done.' Sally closed the heavy lid.

'I mustn't forget my calendar,' said Lizzy remembering it at the last moment. But when she turned again to fetch it from the dressing table she saw it was gone. 'Sally, did you pack it already?'

'No, Miss Benson,' the maid answered. 'I can't say as I've seen it, but don't worry, I expect it'll turn up somewhere, and it'll be found when it wants to be.'

With that, she locked the trunk with a strong padlock, bobbed a curtsey and left the room.

Lizzy moved the dressing table away from the wall, in case the calendar had fallen behind, but it wasn't there and it wasn't underneath the table on the floor. She couldn't find it anywhere - in the bedclothes or in the closet - and even in places she knew it couldn't possibly be. Perhaps Sally was right. In any case, there was nothing she could do; the calendar had simply vanished into thin air.

Mr Collins departed soon after saying how much he regretted the fact that he'd not be seeing them at Christmas. He'd decided to stay in Alton at a lodging house in order to be able to call on Miss Lucas and begin the process of courtship. His patroness, Lady Catherine de Bourgh, understood his wishes to remain until after the seasonal celebrations, but was urging him to leave it no longer than necessary to tie the knot with "dear Miss Lucas" and bring her home to the parsonage at Hunsford. He left with all his usual ceremony and flattery, but Mrs Bennet made it quite clear she had no time for him, practically shooing him out of the door.

'Goodbye, sir,' she said. 'What a pity it is you cannot stay longer, but we are called to Darley Manor in Derbyshire, by my brother Edward. A great estate, by all accounts, what delights we shall enjoy, what diversions we shall experience, I cannot wonder. I am sure you will be most comfortable in your lodgings, though I wonder that Sir William could not find you a bed at Lucas Lodge, or a room at The Swan … he has many connections in Alton, you know.'

'The simple life is one I prefer, Mrs Bennet, and I do not think the Bishop would consider it seemly to be yet sleeping under the same roof as my dearest girl. And though to wait until after Christmas when our two hearts shall be joined as one is both a cruel delay and an inordinately long passage of time, we will after that forever be united in love and felicity.'

Lydia snorted at this, which made Kitty fall about laughing, and left the others staring, unable to think of a single word to say after such a ridiculous outburst. Even Mrs Bennet was momentarily silenced. As soon as he'd gone, the general consensus was that they were all relieved that such protestations and declarations of love would no longer have to be endured. Mr Bennet, who rarely made an appearance out of his study, remarked that he'd never known a finer fellow, and though Collins was not a sensible man, he'd been provided with much amusement and diversion, and was quite sorry to see him go.

With no reason for further delay the journey northwards was soon started. They all piled into Mr Bennet's carriage, which was a bit of a squeeze, and Lizzy couldn't help thinking how different the journey would have been in a modern car. The old carriage bounced along badly made roads, getting stuck once or twice in the snowdrifts that seemed ever higher, the further they travelled. What would have taken a couple of hours became a journey of three days with two overnight stops, staying in inns along the way. Longing for a shower, a hairdryer and a pair of comfy jeans, Lizzy endured it all very well, but was glad, at last, to see the landscape changing to the rugged and dramatic scenery of Derbyshire. At some point along the trail she'd noticed a post chaise following them at some distance. The distinctive yellow carriage rumbled behind, and when she pointed it out to Lizzy, her friend merely smiled and said that was how Miss Austen always travelled for long journeys.

'Is Miss Austen coming to Darley Manor?' asked Lizzy.

'Indeed, the thought of an alternative is quite unthinkable,' Eliza replied, 'for she is always with us ... she would never dream of leaving us behind.'

The implication that Miss Austen was the driving force behind the trip was not lost on Lizzy though she was sure she'd heard Miss Bennet say that it was her uncle who'd invited them all to stay.

Elizabeth added, 'I see what you are thinking, but things are never as they seem.'

No, Lizzy thought, that was certainly true from her experiences so far, and though she was still puzzled by Eliza's comments, she kept them to herself.

They caught a glimpse of Darley Manor before they reached it, a Jacobean house set on high ground and surrounded by woods, the perfect picture of an ancient country house. Mr Bennet told them that the owners, the Bancrofts, had made their fortune as colliery owners in the seventeenth century. The house had been enlarged and extended until it had evolved far beyond its simple beginnings. As they drove down the long drive and up to the door, they saw the housekeeper and servants waiting to welcome them and when Elizabeth exclaimed that her uncle and aunt were standing on the top step to greet them, Lizzy began to feel quite excited.

Chapter 9

Door number *Nine*

Aunt and Uncle Gardiner and their noisy family of six children invited them all in with such good humour that instantly made Lizzy feel very much a part of the proceedings too. There was such excitement as the children, small and large alike, hurled themselves into the arms of their adoring cousins and begged to be played with and twirled about. The house soon swallowed them up, and after Chawton cottage it seemed so large that Lizzy felt she might easily get lost there were so many passages and staircases, some rather strangely leading to nowhere in particular, and others leading to the many floors that housed a multitude of bedrooms.

'I hope you'll like the bedchambers you've been assigned,' said Aunt Gardiner, 'Mrs Robinson knows the house so well, and I know she has picked out the very best.'

'Sister, we are more grateful than we can say for your kind hospitality,' Mrs Bennet answered. 'And what with the disappointments we've had to contend with at home, to be in your society is more pleasure than you can know. I was so sure Jane and Elizabeth were to be married by Valentine's day, and now there's not a sniff of a suitor anywhere … though we've heard Mr Wickham lives nearby. I think you'd like him, such a handsome gentleman.'

Aunt Gardiner was a very astute woman and seeing the distress the conversation was giving to her nieces managed to change it before they'd even reached the top of the staircase.

Lizzy's chamber was large and beautifully furnished with a pink bed upholstered in satin, looking like the sort of smart French bed her mother sighed over in women's magazines. The room's panelled oak walls reminded her of a galleon's interior - she'd once been to see a replica of Sir Francis Drake's *Golden Hinde* whilst on holiday in Devon and had admired the cosy feel of burnished wood and the low ceilings. There was something else which gave her the smallest shock of surprise. When Lizzy noticed the familiar sight of the Christmas calendar, now propped up on the chest of drawers, she remembered Sally's words; that the calendar would turn up when it wanted to and she was filled with a sense of anticipation. In real time several days had passed, but only one of the doors held the flicker of light behind it. The snowman and gardens captured in watercolours in the painting reflected some of the views she could see outside.

Her window looked out onto the gardens and park at the back of the house, a beautiful landscape, which none the less looked rather sad without a single footprint yet upon its snowy surface. It would be a children's paradise, Lizzy thought, and imagined what fun the little Gardiners would have in a garden of this size to explore. When the housekeeper, Mrs Robinson, joined Aunt Gardiner to give them a tour of the house she said that normally there were no children at Darley Manor, that her master, Mr Bancroft, had never married and that the house was to be inherited by a young nephew.

'And is he a local gentleman?' Mrs Bennet asked before the housekeeper managed to draw breath.

Lizzy, Jane and Eliza exchanged glances. Elizabeth was biting her lip hard trying not to laugh. 'Let us hope he does not have the misfortune to call,' she whispered, 'for it is certain my mother will not let him go again until he has proposed to at least one, if not us all!'

'He has a property of his own nearby, Ma'am,' the good housekeeper answered, 'though I believe he is in London for the time being. He is a very busy gentleman, though of the kindest heart and disposition. He calls to see his uncle whenever he can, and is most obliging.'

'There, Mrs Bennet,' Mr Bennet drily commented, 'you can add him to your list of potential suitors.'

Mrs Bennet shot him a warning glance. 'I have no need to do that, sir,' she muttered under her breath. 'I am merely interested in our neighbours, that is all.'

They were shown the saloon, and the drawing room, the dining room and the orangery, every one fitted out in the latest and most fashionable furniture, which drew admiring exclamations from Mrs Bennet and Lydia who delighted in such opulent taste. They had reached the second floor where Mrs Robinson said the picture gallery was a great attraction, housing the portraits of family members through the ages, but though Lizzy would have loved to see them being quite a keen student of art, Mrs Bennet declined, saying she was feeling a little fatigued and would prefer to lie down until the dinner hour.

The party was broken up, and Mrs Robinson thinking her company was no longer required, begged to be excused. The girls were left to their own devices, Mrs Bennet and Aunt Gardiner went their separate ways, and whilst Lydia and Kitty closeted themselves in their room and Mary set off for the library, Lizzy, Jane and Eliza determined on exploring the grounds whose wonderful views beckoned to them through some of the larger French windows. The children latched onto them pulling them by their hands, so excited were they to get out and into the snow. It was like stepping out onto a perfectly iced Christmas cake, like the ones from the baker's in the town where she lived and quite unlike the rough seas Lizzy's darling mum created with a palette knife on their own festive cake. Smooth as a freshly ironed sheet, the snow billowed over the landscape as far as she could see. Pine woods, and great oaks with gnarled trunks and roots, as thick as a man's waist, broke over the surface here and there, stretching away into the hazy distance in lilac mist. The girls left the children happily employed on the upper terrace, descending a stone staircase to step sedately onto the straight paths of the formal gardens. When they came to an iron gate at the end through which they could see the landscape stretching before them, they longed to explore further, but found it was locked. Turning tail, they walked back to the house.

'I always long to make the first mark in the snow,' said Jane echoing Lizzy's thoughts, 'but I'm rather sorry now I have ... there is something so beautiful about an undisturbed vista.'

'Yes,' Eliza agreed, 'and we've well and truly made our mark, though I feel we've been quite restrained. When I was a small child I'd have run circles round the lawn like cousin Henry over there.'

All the girls laughed at that, and just as they were walking up the steps to gain the higher terrace where the children were busy making a snowman, they saw a familiar figure coming from around the side of the house.

'Mr Wickham!' Lizzy exclaimed.

He raised his arm in salute and they watched him lope over in that easy way he had, his handsome face wreathed in smiles.

'When I heard that you were coming, I could not wait to welcome you to Derbyshire, dear ladies,' he said.

'We have only just arrived, Mr Wickham. My goodness, how quickly news travels in this part of the world,' said Elizabeth.

'My mother is currently visiting friends in Hampshire, Miss Elizabeth, and I can assure you there is no faster communicant of information.'

'Now I understand,' she replied with a smile. 'Mothers are very industrious when it comes to relaying news.'

'Yes, indeed, and I am very sorry you will not be able to meet mine at present. Nevertheless, I hope you will be able to accept an invitation to dine the day after tomorrow with your parents and kind aunt and uncle. There will be a little dancing, of course. I thought you'd like to meet some of the people I am proud to call my neighbours.'

'We should be honoured to accept, sir,' Elizabeth answered with no hesitation. Lizzy saw her friend light up when she looked at him. It was an odd thing to consider Mr Wickham as quite opposite a character to the one portrayed in her favourite book, but he certainly seemed very different to how she'd imagined him.

'Then, I shall take it as settled,' he said with a bow. 'I would love to stay and spend more time in your delightful company, but I've guests arriving this very afternoon, and I should hate to miss their coming.'

'Of course,' Elizabeth said, 'we shall look forward to seeing you soon.'

'Until then, dear ladies,' Mr Wickham called, as the girls watched him stride back along the terrace, 'I shall be impatient for your company!'

'Oh, Eliza, I am so happy for you,' said Jane.

'I do not know what you mean, dearest sister.'

'He is so keen … we have not been here half an hour and he is calling so soon.'

'Mr Wickham is being polite, and extending the hospitality due to our mother, that is all.'

'What do you think, Miss Benson?' Jane asked. 'Did Mr Wickham give a sideways look at anyone else?'

Lizzy laughed. 'No, I do not think he was aware of anyone else, but you, dear Miss Elizabeth.'

It was Elizabeth's turn to laugh. 'I shall take no notice of anything else you have to say. I am not so certain of his regard, though I must admit that the more I see him, the more I grow to like him.'

Chapter 10

Door number *Ten*

Everyone went cheerfully to bed that night after the long journey and excitement of the day. When Lizzy awoke next morning she couldn't think where she was at first. It felt strange not to be at the cottage, and such a long way from her mother, but she'd become so used to the extraordinary world she found herself in that she'd stopped questioning what was happening. It was so thrilling to be staying in such a grand house and when the clock on the mantelpiece struck six with a tinkling strike of bells she knew she would have to get up and explore, just as soon as she'd opened her calendar, a daily ritual which was giving her more pleasure than she'd ever dreamed possible.

Door number ten opened easily, and Lizzy was drawn instantly into the world beyond by its subject matter and vivid colours. The little painting was exquisitely detailed and when she looked more closely she could see a long gallery of the kind she remembered her teachers at school describing as an entertainment space for the richly dressed Elizabethans who promenaded in stiff farthingales and ruffs, dripping in jewels and precious stones. Indeed, the room was decorated with paintings hanging on the walls, and incredibly, she could see the tiny details of every one. Her eye was drawn to a painting of a young girl dressed in black, her stiff stomacher enlivened only by an ornate gold cross, but rather severe until a froth of pleated ruff and diaphanous wings above it softened and framed her beautiful face. Her hair was curly and caught behind a string of gleaming pearls. The only other adornment was a single red rose she held between a finger and her thumb. She looked a lot like a portrait of Mary, Queen of Scots, that she'd once seen in the National Portrait Gallery in London and Lizzy remembered how she'd been touched to her heart by the sad tale of the young queen.

A voice in her ear startled her. 'Do you ever wish you could go back in time and change history, Miss Benson?'

Curiously, and weirder still, she felt herself shrinking, as she had done once before, and in the next second she found herself standing in the painting, as large as life. It was a moment or two before she could speak. One minute she'd been sitting on her bed with the calendar in her hand, the next she was through the door itself. The picture gallery stretched before her, rush matting under her feet and diamond paned windows illuminating the space on every side. It was an empty room except for the paintings along one panelled wall, of course, and the occasional chair or oak chest bearing a bowl of dried lavender, which emitted sweet fragrance like an Elizabethan pomander.

When she turned to answer the girl at her side, she knew exactly whom she must be. There was a strong resemblance to both Elizabeth and Jane; they could have been taken for sisters. It was the girl she'd seen crossing the yard at the back of Chawton cottage, it could be no one else but Miss Jane Austen.

'Oh yes, Miss Austen,' she replied, 'I heartily wish I could go back and intervene, persuade Queen Elizabeth that she was making a big mistake, and stop her signing Mary's death warrant.'

'I knew you were a girl after my own heart, and if I could save poor Mary's life from the executioner's hands, I would too. She was so maligned, an innocent girl used by those in power above her. But, nothing changes very much, does it, Miss Benson, though I think there have been remarkable changes in your time, if I am correct?'

Lizzy could hardly believe she was standing next to Jane Austen, her greatest heroine and the author of her favourite books.

'Undoubtedly, though in many ways women are slaves to convention as much as ever we were. We might have the choice of splendid careers that you could not have dreamed of, but it is still difficult for women to juggle both a profession and a family life, not that I have to worry about that myself yet.'

'You are to be a school teacher, I believe.'

'Yes, I've recently finished my training and I'm looking forward to starting at a school in my town after Christmas.'

'You are very brave, Miss Benson. Though I adore small children, I could not imagine being a teacher. When I think of the poor women who suffered in my youth at the hands of their pupils. But, I daresay it will be different for you. Your pupils will adore you and greedily eat up the crumbs of knowledge you feed them!'

'I certainly hope so.'

'Perhaps you think me unfeeling, but I have my reasons. I have a little experience of time travelling, and found myself forced to be a governess once and that was quite enough. Though all was resolved to my satisfaction at the finish.'

Lizzy's eyes met Jane's and she saw the famed hazel eyes twinkle with amusement.

'Now tell me, Miss Benson, what do you think of *First Impressions*? It requires a little editing, I think.'

Suddenly, it all fell into place. It wasn't *Pride and Prejudice* after all that she was watching unfold, leaf by leaf, like an enchanted fan revealing its story in pictures, though very like it in places. It was *First Impressions*, the book Jane Austen had written when she'd been about the same age as Lizzy, and falling in love for the first time with a young Irishman by the name of Tom Lefroy. Somehow, Lizzy decided, she was being given an opportunity to look through a window or in this case, beyond the many doors into the mind of a writer at work. And not just into any novelist's imagination, but the one who mattered most to her in the world.

'I am enjoying it very much!' she answered, aware that Miss Austen was scrutinising her expression.

'I wrote it many years ago, Miss Benson. I started it, at least the imagining of it one Christmas, when I was rather in love with a young man who went on to break my heart. But, I have a feeling you know that little part of my history, and it is partly why I need your advice.'

'You need my advice?' Lizzy could hardly believe her ears.

'I've lost my way a little with the plot, and I'm not sure how to get it back. Oh, I know it will get there in the end. I know my book will be published, and it will be a work of far greater significance than this one would be, were it to be published, but I feel there is something missing.'

Lizzy nodded and was about to speak when Jane stopped her. 'No, don't tell me, Miss Benson. You understand, it just will not work if you give me the answer ... I must work it out for myself.'

'Of course,' Lizzy replied. 'Am I able to give you any clues?'

'Perhaps the merest hint of what I'm missing, Miss Benson. I feel very strongly that there is something missing.'

'Yes!' Lizzy exclaimed, bursting to be able to tell her. 'There is something ... or someone missing.'

'Dash it all - I knew it! It's a someone who has not yet introduced themselves. My characters are always springing out of nowhere; believe me, I have little control over them, but sometimes they are reticent to show themselves. Tell me, is this person of a shy disposition?'

'That's a tricky question, Miss Austen, and I fear I may give away too much if I answer it.'

'Now, I beg you, Miss Benson, no names. Come along, while we consider what to do next ... we will promenade, as Mary liked to do. Take my arm and perhaps inspiration will strike.'

They set off along the gallery, arm in arm, with a decided view to admire the paintings, Lizzy mentally pinching herself in disbelief. It was almost impossible to think she was chatting away to Jane Austen as if she were an old friend, and feeling the warmth of her arm through her muslin sleeve, but the whole event was utterly bizarre. The first half dozen pictures they admired were similar to the painting of Mary; Tudor portraits of men and women wearing extraordinary clothing. The men, in particular, seemed to amuse Jane with their pumpkin shaped breeches and cod-pieces on display. Then after that, came a series of ladies in sackback gowns, satin shining and gathered in cascading folds to the floor. Gentlemen in long peruke wigs followed with their ladies in dresses so wide that Lizzy wondered how they'd managed to move around. With their hair towering high above them, powdered, be-ribboned and festooned with roses, she was reminded of Beatrix Potter's tiny mice in her Christmas tale where they hid in teacups from the tailor's cat.

There was one portrait that arrested their attention and made them stop dead in their tracks. Towards the other end of the gallery they came across a full-length portrait of a young man. Recently painted, the smell of oil paint was so fresh that it hung in the air. He was very handsome, dressed for the outdoors in hues of green, which melded into the landscape of trees and the Derbyshire hills around him. In the background was a house they recognised - Darley Manor.

'I have a feeling I know who this might be,' said Lizzy. 'Perhaps this gentleman is the nephew of Mr Gardiner's client - the housekeeper mentioned him. He is to inherit.'

'Oh, I see,' said Jane, stepping forward to inspect the picture more closely. 'He is rather good-looking, and would make a credible hero. Rich too, which is always an excellent quality in suitable gentlemen. Is there a name on it?'

Lizzy caught her breath when she saw the plaque. 'There is a name, Miss Austen, and one I like rather well.'

She didn't think she ought to say any more and feared she might have said too much when Miss Austen didn't reply. Jane stood with her arms crossed, looking the gentleman up and down, drawing in large breaths and sighing rather a lot.

'Hmm,' she said at last. 'I suppose Darcy has a certain ring to it, though I'd rather fancied an Irish name, yet to be perfectly honest I haven't thought of anything so romantic as this one. And he's certainly got the look of a man from that part of the world with those grey eyes and dark mane of hair.'

Lizzy watched her and knew she wasn't thinking about the man in the painting. She looked far away in another time and space, and for a second her eyes were misted with tears.

'He'll do,' Miss Austen said at last. 'I think he's the one I've been looking for, though I've got too many heroes at the moment. It's no good, one of them will have to be bad ... might as well be him.'

Lizzy wanted to call out and ask her to re-consider, but she'd promised not to interfere, and surely Miss Austen would figure it out for herself, wouldn't she? As she opened her mouth to speak again, she started to feel rather unwell. Lizzy felt her stomach roll over, a very strange sensation, as if she was descending in the department store lift at John Lewis's, plummeting down through the bowels of the earth leaving everything behind above her. She reached for a chair to sit down, closing her eyes in an attempt to stem the overwhelming feeling of nausea that rushed over her, and when she opened them again, she was sitting on the bed, just as if nothing had happened. It took her a few minutes to get back her breath and when she'd recovered, she looked back at the tiny door in the calendar, which she swore she'd just passed through. Right in the far corner of the gallery seated at a table in front of the portrait sat Miss Austen, a quill in her hand. Head bowed, and writing rapidly, it was clear she'd found the inspiration she was looking for.

Chapter 11

Door number *Eleven*

The excitement was too much for Mr Bennet. With Mr Gardiner gone early to Lambton on business, he was being subjected to what he considered to be an onslaught of females. When his daughters, his wife and sister-in-law, along with their friend Miss Benson started discussing shoe roses and ribbons at the breakfast table with their other female relations he decided to leave for the library as soon as he could, a far grander room than his own study back at Chawton, so he knew he would be free to enjoy himself. There he would remain undisturbed, amongst the leather bound volumes, and if he were lucky, nobody would notice if he was gone all day.

'I hope Mr Wickham will like your feet, girls, after all the trouble you're going to in order for him to notice them,' he said, rising from his chair and dabbing at his mouth with a napkin.

Elizabeth chuckled at his observation. 'Papa, our toes are as important as the curls on our head when it comes to a ball. Every detail must be talked of and discussed. I hope you've given much thought over to the matter of which dancing shoes you are to wear.'

'Lizzy, I am thankful that I do not have such elaborate and perplexing dilemmas to add to my daily burdens. I possess just one pair that your mama procured shortly before our wedding nuptials, and they are all I need. And in order to keep them looking just as new as the day I was presented with them, I've made it a rule never to dance unless absolutely necessary.'

This produced an outburst from his wife, who declared she'd never heard a word truer said. 'I hope you will break the habit of a lifetime, Mr Bennet, and let them see some wear this evening.'

'On that, dear madam, I assure you, no such custom will be broken. I hardly like to have the attention taken from our dear daughters - I fear that an exhibition from me may prompt such a diversion on the spectacle that their protracted efforts for ensnaring the opposite sex will all come to naught.'

They watched him leave the room, Mrs Bennet still remonstrating with him from her chair whilst Lydia and Kitty looked nonplussed. Elizabeth and Jane were still laughing at his sense of humour, which hardly ever altered they said, telling Lizzy how he loved to tease them all.

The occupations of the day were set, and the evening could not come too soon for any of the girls. They took a walk around the park in the afternoon to try and make the time pass faster, and discovered that the gate was now open and they could explore beyond the confines of the gardens. Away beyond the woods and down in the valley they could see the nearby village of Lambton, smoke rising in curls from the chimneys of the golden stone of the tiny houses. Lydia and Kitty said they longed to find the nearest milliner's, and they all agreed that a walk to the village very soon would be a prospect to which they all looked forward.

As they walked along taking in the glorious views from all around they noticed on the opposite side of the valley a large, handsome stone house, standing well on rising ground, and backed by a ridge of high woody hills.

'I wonder who lives there,' said Elizabeth, 'in such a beautiful building.'

'Perhaps it is someone we might meet this evening,' added Jane, 'Mr Wickham said he was inviting all his friends and neighbours.'

'Knowing our luck, the owner of such a house is very likely to be old and married,' said Lydia.

'In any case, such a man of wealth is unlikely to be interested in any of us,' said Jane. 'We have only our charms for a dowry, and for most gentleman of fortune that simply is not enough.'

Lizzy could see Jane looked most upset and knew she must be thinking of Mr Bingley. Elizabeth noticed also, and taking her sister's arm she patted it reassuringly. 'I do not think that is the case for all gentlemen, Jane. Mr Bingley, I am certain, is not so shallow.'

Jane smiled at her sister, but only sighed. Lizzy hoped something might happen to bring Mr Bingley back into her sphere, but she could not foresee any change in the present circumstances.

Lizzy found her gown laid out for her on the bed and when one of the housemaids came to help her, she thought about Sally and hoped she was having a good holiday whilst they were away. She was sure the young housemaid enjoyed little leisure and for all she knew was still having to work hard and run errands, but she couldn't help thinking about her and hoping she'd enjoy a little festive fun whilst they were all away. There was little time for reflection, however, and now the evening was getting started, time was passing like sand running through the glass of an egg timer.

The excitement was palpable as they clambered into the carriages and set off for their party. Even Lizzy left off her usual reserve, and declared she could quite get used to the stunning scenery in the area as the carriages bowled down the lanes to their destination.

Mr Wickham welcomed them to Holmeshaw Hall with great enthusiasm, introducing the Bennets and the Gardiners to all his friends. As they moved round the room Lizzy searched every countenance in the hope of seeing Mr Darcy, and when, at last, she heard Mr Wickham pronounce his name, she could hardly believe her ears and eyes. However, he was not quite the man she was expecting to see. In appearance he was everything the portrait had promised, but his manner was such, that she could not have felt more surprised. He smiled and bowed; he was lively and interested in everything and everyone. He was not the proud man the Bennets knew in *Pride and Prejudice*, but congenial and obliging, unassuming and humble. Lizzy couldn't help watching Elizabeth for any sign of interest in the gentleman, but saw none. Indeed, she only appeared to have eyes for Mr Wickham.

'Miss Bennet, Mr Wickham tells me you reside near Alton?' Mr Darcy enquired of her.

Elizabeth, who had been watching Mr Wickham talking to a pretty young lady with auburn hair turned to answer. 'Yes, we live at Chawton, but two miles from Alton.'

'I have heard the Hampshire countryside is very pretty,' he continued, 'and if its residents are a reflection of its beauties, it must be a handsome county.'

'It is pleasing enough, Mr Darcy, though has little of the dramatic scenery one sees in Derbyshire. Hampshire is the county of my birth, and there is nowhere else I feel so at home. As for its residents, I daresay many a county boasts its share of pleasing inhabitants whose attractive qualities are exaggerated into beauty by flattering attentions.'

'Eliza, do not run on so,' her mother began. 'Mr Darcy is paying you a great compliment, I am sure.'

'I am sorry if I have offended, Miss Bennet, but I always speak the truth. Before you came into Derbyshire my friend, Mr Wickham, spoke of you and your sisters as being the prettiest girls he ever met in his life.'

Elizabeth looked slightly more cheered by that disclosure, but seemed irritated at the same time. 'And is that all Derbyshire gentlemen consider when becoming acquainted with a young woman? What of our minds, Mr Darcy? I suppose we can be as stupid as you like so long as we are pretty enough creatures.'

'Believe me, Miss Bennet, we are quite prepared to fall in love with wit and intelligence, as well as a handsome face. I have heard it said that the eyes are a mirror of brilliance, and have often meditated on the very great pleasure, which a pair of fine eyes in the face of a pretty woman can bestow.

Yours are uncommonly fine.'

'Thank the kind gentleman, Eliza! What a pretty way you have with words, sir,' said Mrs Bennet. ' I do not like to boast of my daughters' beauty, but they are uncommonly handsome. Jane, my eldest, is usually the one that gentlemen seem to notice on first acquaintance … you have met her, I suppose? But, all my girls have qualities enough to satisfy, I would hope.'

'Mother, please … look everyone is going into dinner.' Elizabeth immediately took the arms of her sister Jane and Lizzy to march them in the opposite direction. 'Good heavens, did you ever hear anything like it? If there is one thing I cannot bear it is a gentleman who flatters without sincerity, and on the first occasion of introduction. Indeed, is there anything more off-putting than the sort of flummery employed by those who have no intention of looking beyond one's outward appearance? Mr Darcy is worse than Mr Collins for possessing the talent of flattering with delicacy.'

'I thought he was a very pleasant gentleman, if a little effusive,' said Jane. 'A rich man looking for a wife may have few opportunities to attract the woman he desires especially if she does not normally reside in his county. Perhaps he strikes while the iron is hot!'

Elizabeth laughed at that and agreed that might well be a possibility but that she would avoid him wherever she could if that really was his sole motive. 'I am not ready to marry a man who will fall in love with me for my fine eyes alone. I want someone to love me for who I am, not just because I am beautiful.'

Jane and Lizzy both laughed in reply. 'Well, I am sure Mr Wickham is your man, in that case,' said Jane. 'I do not believe I ever heard you say that he mentioned your lovely countenance, though if what Mr Darcy says is true, it seems clear he has spoken of you in those terms.'

'And which I find perfectly acceptable. To hear of such pleasing attentions third-hand is all I could hope for, and I am exceedingly flattered! I must admit, Mr Wickham is an exceptionally fine young man.'

At dinner, they took their places at the long table, and Lizzy could see immediately that Elizabeth was unhappy at being seated next to Mr Darcy. To further discompose her Mr Wickham's attention was completely given up to the young lady he'd spent so much time talking to earlier. Lizzy sat on Mr Darcy's other side, but the seat next to her was empty. Mr Darcy made polite conversation every now and again, but then seemed only to want to talk to Elizabeth. Hardly had she started to feel that the dinner was to be a long affair with no one to talk to than the entrance of someone Lizzy recognised too well, made her sit up and start in her chair with surprise.

'Mr Williams!' cried Mr Wickham, standing to greet him with a hearty handshake. 'You made better progress than I thought ... how splendid! Dear friends, here is my neighbour, Mr Williams, all the way from London and prepared to make merry with us all. Let me see you to your chair, sir.'

He was hardly fit for merriment, Lizzy decided, if his former behaviour was anything to go by, but she had to admit he did not appear to be quite as formidable and severe as she had seen him in Chawton. Mr Williams really was very good-looking, she thought. He looked taller than ever, and his dark hair, which gleamed like the black of night, waved back from the strong features of his face. In candlelight his eyes sparkled, and when she caught him glancing in her direction she could not explain the momentary tug on her heart as his eyes met hers. Such a physical response caught her completely off guard, she could not explain it and inwardly scolded herself.

He spent the first ten minutes engaged in conversation with the lady on his other side and completely ignored her, which made Lizzy feel rather cross, as she'd never heard him string more than three or four words in a sentence when talking to her. Mr Darcy uttered a couple of polite enquiries in her way, but was so taken up with trying and failing to impress Elizabeth, that for all his efforts Lizzy started to wish she could be anywhere else. Looking round the table everyone else seemed to be having such a good time. Mr Wickham seemed totally mesmerised by the lady whose name he kept pronouncing loudly. Miss King was pretty, but not a patch on Elizabeth, and Lizzy felt really worried when she remembered the part Mary King had played in *Pride and Prejudice*, not that she need be necessarily perturbed.

Nothing was going the way she expected, and the story as she knew it was completely altered. Lydia and Kitty seemed happy enough. They were flirting outrageously with a couple of Mr Wickham's redcoat comrades, and laughing at everything they said. Jane looked less entertained though the young man who was trying hard to gain her attention seemed pleasant enough. She was still in love with Mr Bingley, that was clear, and no one would be able to distract or persuade her otherwise.

Mr Williams turned to address her at last.

'Miss Benson, how do you like Derbyshire?'

'I like it very well, Mr Williams, though I've not been here long enough to see very much of it.'

'I believe it is the finest country in all England, and beyond comparison with London. But, I suppose you would not like to live here after being used to the entertainment of a big city.'

'It has always been a great wish of mine to live in the country, Mr Williams. There are some very pretty houses in the villages that I couldn't help wondering about as we passed by. I am fascinated by other people's lives. Do you ever wonder about how the people came to live in a specific house or how they arrived in a particular village?'

'I suppose I never thought about it much before. Have you wondered about Darley Manor's neighbour then, Miss Benson?'

'Are you referring to the large mansion we saw at the back of the house?' Lizzy asked. 'Do you know who lives there?'

'Well, I should hope so.'

'It must be someone very rich,' Lizzy said with a smile. 'Do tell, Mrs Bennet is longing to know!'

'I am not certain if I should tell you, after all,' he said mysteriously, his mouth twitching.

Lizzy could hardly believe that she was almost having a proper conversation with Mr Williams. His sentences were hardly longer than usual but his manner was a little more animated, and he appeared to have a teasing smile just playing at the corner of his lips. Her eyes flickered over his mouth, and he smiled showing his pearl-white teeth.

'Does the house belong to someone we know here?' Lizzy asked thinking he was playing a game with her. 'Let me see if I can guess.'

'The house is mine, Miss Benson.'

She was so shocked she just blurted out. 'The house is *yours*, Mr Williams? Are you talking about the house up on the hill that you can see at the back of Darley Manor?'

'Yes, my family have owned Amberley for several generations.'

Lizzy giggled. 'It sounds a bit like Pemberley.'

'The names of the houses in this area all have a similar sound, I suppose. Darley, Amberley and Pemberley ... 'ley' means a clearing in a woodland, and if you notice all the houses are set amongst trees. Pemberley is a particularly fine example.'

Mr Darcy turned at that moment to address her. 'Did I hear mention of Pemberley? I hope now I am returned to Derbyshire, once more, that I shall open the house up to visitors. Miss Benson, I hope you will accept an invitation ... I shall speak to Mr and Mrs Bennet forthwith.'

'That would be delightful,' she answered, thinking that if she could get Elizabeth inside Pemberley that might be a way forward.

She looked again to Mr Williams who seemed to have turned back into his usual sulky self. She made a few more attempts at conversation but he'd withdrawn, transformed into the character she knew well, and he just ignored her, preferring to toy with the food on his plate.

After dinner they enjoyed some dancing, and Lizzy noticed that Elizabeth managed to dance with Mr Wickham twice, which made her very happy, and once with Mr Darcy, which seemed to have the opposite effect. Mr Williams refrained from joining in any of the dancing. He stood at the side looking as stern as ever, which made Lizzy feel very cross for reasons she couldn't readily explain. She was finding it hard to fathom him out. Every time she seemed to be getting somewhere with him, even if it was just engaging him in a little more conversation, he would block her out again.

Sometimes he appeared to be looking at her but bore such an angry expression she was made to feel very uncomfortable. Lizzy was still thinking about him on the journey home and even when she climbed the grand old staircase to bed, she could not get him out of her thoughts.

When she entered her room, it was glowing with the luminous light coming from the little doorway in the calendar. She'd forgotten all about it that morning, and now she rushed to see what was inside. It came as no surprise to see the tiny painting of Amberley Hall, but what astonished her more was the figure of a man on horseback riding up to the great door as if his life depended upon it. But, just as he reached it, she saw him bring his steed to a halt, whereupon he turned in his saddle and looked straight at her to doff his cap. As she stared, the figure came closer into view until she knew beyond a doubt that it was Mr Williams she saw, looking very handsome in his cape. When he blew her a kiss, she was certain she must have imagined it, as in the next second he disappeared altogether in a gallop into the far distance, and all that was left was the handsome stone building rising out of the trees.

Chapter 12

Door number *Twelve*

The next day brought Mr Darcy himself with the invitation he'd promised for an evening party that very night. Mrs Bennet and Mrs Gardiner were effusive in their praise of him.

'Now, sister, do you not think he might suit Jane?' Mrs Bennet asked.

'I think he might suit any of your daughters, Mrs Bennet, though he seems to have a marked preference for Eliza. He could hardly take his eyes off her.'

'Yes, but she declares she does not like him. Mr Wickham is her man, though I have reason to suspect he is by no means decided in a partner for life.'

'Whatever do you mean, my dear?'

'Well, for all the attention he has been paying my Elizabeth, did you not notice that he spent most of the time talking to that Mary King. I think that's her name, the large-boned, ungainly girl with the freckles.'

'He danced with her three times, I think.'

'Four! And when I made enquiries I discovered she has recently come into an inheritance.'

'I see, and when all things are considered, you are most likely correct to have your suspicions.'

'It is enough to vex me,' said Mrs Bennet, 'and now that nice Mr Darcy seems interested, I know Lizzy will not have him, she is so inclined to be perverse, and Jane is too lovestruck to care about anyone. Mr Williams might do for either one, but he's such a proud gentleman and so stuck up in his ways. I declare I do not know what shall become of us all.'

'I should not worry, too much, I am certain all will work out for the best. My nieces are so beautiful and such adorable creatures that some kind gentleman will see their delightful qualities ... they cannot fail to have young men fall in love with them. And you never know, perhaps Mr Bingley may come to his senses yet.'

Mrs Bennet could not be placated, even with all the soothing words her sister-in-law offered. Mrs Gardiner could only hope that something might happen soon to set matters right.

Mr Darcy's residence, Pemberley Manor, was all that they had expected and more. It was a large house, but still maintained the feel of a family home despite its elegance. It was warm and comfortable, and although wishing to remain completely unimpressed by it, Elizabeth admitted to Jane and Lizzy that she rather liked what she saw. Mrs Bennet was particularly effusive in her praise as they entered the house, urging Jane and Elizabeth to regard its architecture, furnishings and number of rooms.

Mr Darcy greeted them cordially and introduced them to his sister, Miss Georgiana, and his aunt, Lady Catherine de Bourgh, who had arrived from London that very morning. The young lady was very welcoming, but the elder sat imperiously, hardly acknowledging any of them. Mr Wickham came in then with some of his party, which included Miss King, causing much bustle and another diversion, and with the arrival of Mr Williams the room was soon full.

Tea was served, and at Lady Catherine's instigation, a suggestion for the ladies to exhibit their skills upon the pianoforte ensued.

'I love to hear music played well,' she said. 'All young ladies have the benefit of such excellent lessons these days, though my poor daughter who suffers much illness has been unable to take the best advantage of the fine musicians to be found in London. I have left her there in the care of her nurse who attends her day and night. I am always wanted elsewhere and my counsel desired so much that I have been forced to come away. My nephew needs me so much, and to him I am always obliging.'

Mr Darcy looked rather surprised at that statement but smiled as if ready to agree with her every word.

'I am sorry to hear your daughter is unwell. What ails her, your ladyship?' said Mrs Bennet, as curious as ever about everyone's business.

'My physicians have never been able to satisfactorily discover what is at the root of her illness, Mrs Bennet. Since her birth she was a delicate creature, and prone to chills. We kept her swaddled for the first year of her life, but nothing improved her health, and so it has been ever since.'

'Perhaps her health would be improved in the country air, your ladyship,' Mrs Bennet ventured. 'Would she not be better in Derbyshire?'

'That is not the advice I have been given and I have consulted the best of physicians. Fresh air might carry her off altogether, they tell me. Warm fires and small apartments in winter will see her through, and then she will perhaps be able to return in the spring. Now, who will play first? Georgiana, you will set the standard, I think!'

Miss Darcy, a rather timid and shy girl, reluctantly stood to cross the room to the pianoforte. Elizabeth, seeing her distress, volunteered to turn her music sheets, and at once, relief flooded Georgiana's features. She played extremely well, Lizzy thought, as she observed Miss Darcy, and hoped no one would ask her to play. She'd never had a proper lesson in her life before, and though she'd tried to learn some period pieces by watching YouTube videos, she had to admit, she was not a true proficient! She couldn't help noticing how Mr Darcy could not take his eyes off Eliza. It was very clear he admired her, and when his sister stopped playing he offered to escort

Elizabeth back to her seat. She reluctantly took his hand, all the while staring in Mr Wickham's direction. He was oblivious to Miss Bennet, being in deep conversation with Miss King. Lizzy wished Mr Darcy were not so attentive. She was sure Eliza would like him better if he were a little less gushing. If only she could speak to Miss Austen again, and hint that Elizabeth did not admire a man that fawned.

Jane played next. Whilst not as talented a performer as Georgiana, her style and sweet manner won over the audience, and several of the young men made a beeline to escort her to her chair. Flattered by the attention, nevertheless, she still retained a look of sadness, an expression Lizzy knew would only be removed by the sight of the one person she wished to see.

'Miss Elizabeth, I hope you will play next,' Mr Darcy declared, 'We are longing to hear you perform.'

'Then I am certain to disappoint, Mr Darcy.'

'You could never do that, dear lady. Besides, I am sure you play very well.'

'I hope my performance will be adequate, but I would hate to set myself up for censure. If I convince you of low expectations, I might then persuade you of my brilliance, or at least, of playing a passable tune.'

Everyone laughed. Elizabeth sat down at the pianoforte and began to play. She sang too, so sweetly, that any deficiency in her playing was made up for by the tone of her voice. There were calls for more after she finished, and so she obliged once more with another song.

Mr Wickham joined her then, and Elizabeth positively glowed with pleasure. Miss King found a companion in one of Mr Wickham's officer friends, and Mr Darcy merely took up his station at the mantelpiece to observe.

'Miss Benson,' he said, 'we have not heard you play.'

'Oh, Mr Darcy,' Lizzy replied anxiously, 'I do not usually play in public.'

'Then now is as good a time to start as any,' came the bellowing voice of Lady Catherine. 'You will never become a true proficient if you do not perform for company.'

Lizzy wished the ground would swallow her up. But when Lady Catherine chided her once more, she felt she had no choice but to get up. Sitting down at the pianoforte, her mind went blank. Of all the pieces she had ever played the only one that kept coming into her mind was the signature tune from her favourite *Pride and Prejudice* film. It was quite a tricky piece and she knew she'd probably forgotten parts of it, but she managed to fudge her way through it. At one point she looked up to see Mr Williams staring at her so intently that she was nearly put off altogether. By some miracle she managed to get to the end without making too many mistakes and was completely surprised by the burst of spontaneous applause that erupted afterwards.

'With a little more practise you might do better, but that was quite an accomplished performance, Miss Benson,' said Lady Catherine. 'I do not know the piece - do enlighten us as to the composer.'

'His name is Marinelli, ma'am. I believe he was trying to evoke the early hours of the day with this piece of music.'

'Oh, an Italian ... they are unsurpassed in their composition, but I have never heard of *him*.'

'No, Lady Catherine, I understand he is quite a modern composer.'

'I believe I am au fait with the latest and very best of new music, Miss Benson. I daresay he does not frequent the circles to which I belong.'

'No, I'm sure not,' admitted Lizzy, feeling both chastened and amused by her own thoughts.

Declining further requests to play, she quickly found her seat once more. Elizabeth was very effusive in her praise.

'You must teach me that piece; it is exquisite. I never saw a room so transfixed, though when I say room, I have to observe there was one person who seemed completely absorbed in your playing.'

'I cannot think who you mean, Miss Eliza.'

'Mr Williams could not take his eyes off you. I never saw him so enraptured.'

'Come now, Elizabeth, I think you're teasing me,' said Lizzy with a little chuckle. 'I only saw him watching in his usual cross and haughty manner. Anyway, you have your share of admirers. Mr Wickham and Mr Darcy will end up duelling over you if their behaviour is anything to go by.'

'I do not share your appraisal, Miss Benson. Mr Wickham is being polite, I think. He's made his preference very plain, and discovering that Miss King has recently inherited a vast fortune puts paid to any chances I might have had with that gentleman. As for Mr Darcy, I am certain his interest is only in gaining a spouse, and hence acquiring a brood mare. He has no real interest in the person I am. He sees a girl who might do, someone he is vaguely attracted to, but I know the minute he discovers I am penniless he will look elsewhere even if he is desperate for an heir.'

'Mr Darcy looks at you as if he is falling in love with you,' Lizzy urged.

'And I have met the type before, Miss Benson. He is a flirt, and a flatterer of women, and he will have to prove himself more worthy if he is to gain my heart.'

Lizzy smiled. 'Do you think first impressions are fixed? What will it take for you to change your mind about him?'

'First impressions are a very valuable guide, I think, Miss Benson. I have studied the gentleman in question and I am sure I have the measure of him.'

Lizzy couldn't help thinking that Miss Austen had lost the plot. If only there was some way she could help to get her back on track.

Everyone agreed that they'd enjoyed a very pleasant evening on the whole; though Elizabeth made some arch remarks about Mr Darcy and Mr Wickham being disappointing company, and Lizzy couldn't help remarking on Mr Williams's behaviour. He'd spent most of the time sitting by himself, ignoring attempts at conversation even when Lizzy tried her very best to engage him, though why she continued to bother, she was beginning to wonder.

It was very late by the time they got back to Darley Manor, and Lizzy couldn't wait to see if the Advent calendar would be lit up in the usual way. With great excitement she saw the door of number twelve glowing, and peeling back the door saw a scene she recognised immediately. It looked just like the ending of one of her favourite films. She could see a beautiful landscape wreathed in early morning mist, with a little bridge crossing a stream in the foreground and a young girl who could only be Elizabeth Bennet walking along looking dreamily about her. In the distance, a figure of a man loomed, striding along in breeches, his white shirt undone and his cape flowing back behind him. Lizzy peered closely at the pictures because there was something so familiar about the lady and the gentleman, but the little film was so small it was hard to make their features out. She squinted and holding up the calendar nearer to her eyes felt the oddest sensation.

As if she were standing in the long grass, she shivered with the cold and pulled her pelisse closer, wrapping herself in its warmth. Early morning smells of dew and wet grass assailed her senses, she heard a cacophony of birdsong, and her heart was filled with such feelings as she'd never experienced before. Her stomach rolled over as she watched the gentleman come closer. He was so very handsome, and the feelings that overcame her left her reeling with happiness. In a moment he was by her side, and had swept her into his arms before she could say a word. His eyes held hers and the look that passed between them needed no wordy explanation. His arms were strong, and she felt safe, a feeling of coming home. Lizzy felt his fingers stroke her face, and then as he tilted her chin towards him, she felt his lips on hers. They were soft, he kissed her tenderly and she was so lost in the moment, that when she opened her eyes, she could not believe what she was seeing. He smiled for just a second, before the image faded in the blink of an eye, and she found herself back with a jolt in her cosy chamber. Lizzy screwed up her eyes in an effort to rid herself of the picture of his good-looking countenance, but she could still see him in her mind's eye. She hardly dared look at the little painting for she had an idea exactly who it was that she'd kissed with such sweetness. As she opened one eye to steal a glance, a miniature portrait of a gentleman she knew only too well stared back. Mr Williams, looking more handsome than ever, was standing at the side of a bridge in a misty landscape, waving to her. Her mouth gaped open in shock, and she looked away hardly wanting to see what was there. When she plucked up the courage to look once more, he was gone, and the sense of disappointment overwhelmed her. Touching her lips, she could still feel the sensation of those others, but she hardly dared acknowledge the emotions that made her heart beat just a little faster.

Chapter 13

Door number *Thirteen*

When Lizzy woke next morning, she knew some kind maid had been in the early hours to make the fire in her room, even so there was such a chill that her nose felt blue with cold. The curtains were drawn apart to show the whitening world outside, but the windows were so frosted with ferns of ice, as if a fairy hand had painted them, that it was impossible to see out. Grabbing her dressing gown, Lizzy wrapped herself up, pulling on long socks before venturing across the room. Scratching a tiny hole through the sparkling ice, fashioned in fronds and leaves, she could see that snow had fallen heavily in the night. Icicles hung from the roof ledge above, dangling in spears for Jack Frost to arm himself. There was so much to see through the window, snow-covered hills and peaks stretching away, and the glimpse of a lake surrounded by pine trees. It was just possible to see Amberley Manor on its high ridge in the distance, plumes of blue smoke rising into the grey sky, which reminded Lizzy of the calendar. She picked it up from the chest of drawers, and couldn't help taking another peek at the door she'd opened the night before.

It had turned back into a painting; there wasn't so much as a flake of falling snow drifting from the still sky, though it now looked as if the landscape in the picture had also suffered a heavy snowfall. There were no visible footprints in the snow, and as much as she looked, she could not see any evidence of anyone ever being there, least of all the man who now occupied her thoughts. She couldn't imagine why he did so with such disturbing frequency because the real Mr Williams she knew and disliked; irritated her beyond belief. It was clear she'd been in some sort of ridiculous trance the day before, and the only experience she could compare it with was one of having an inexplicable dream, as she occasionally had, where some guy she normally didn't like turned into the person she was kissing. For some very weird reason she couldn't begin to comprehend, Mr Williams had become a kind of Darcy-like figure, fleetingly, when she'd fallen into a trance-like state with the calendar still in her hand. That was the only possible reason she could have enjoyed the kiss, she told herself, and tried to stop thinking about the sensations it had on her whole being. It had been so delicious, and the shock to find Mr Williams gazing at her had been too much to contemplate.

With trembling fingers, she opened the door of number thirteen, and the exact same number of tiny Christmas cards fell out, small enough for a dolls' house, all with beautifully painted scenes of Georgian Christmases long ago. Lizzy knew the Victorians had first made the cards popular so they were not around in Jane Austen's day, but each one gave a glimpse of a pretty Regency tableaux with landscapes and figures. There were illustrations of Christmas parties, games of blind man's buff, and young men stealing kisses from unsuspecting girls who just happened to be standing under boughs of glistening mistletoe pearls. Other cards showed countryside inns, coaches and horses in the snow, filled to overflowing with passengers journeying home to loved ones, with the coachman cracking the whip and sounding the horn. There were robins and snowmen, horse-drawn sleighs and green holly, dancing girls and boys in best Christmas gowns and frock-coats kicking up the chalk on the ballroom floor. Some were scented with rosewater, others glittered with tinsel or spangles, there were embossed cards bearing red satin bows, and one even had a silver charm under the picture of a plum pudding. Every card was a delight, but Lizzy quickly found a favourite. A little larger than the rest, the card was like a tiny theatre with flaps either side, and decorated with pine trees powdered by snow and garlanded with lanterns, which glowed in the winter's light. When they were pulled aside, there was a frozen lake and a skating party illustrated, with young men and women gliding over the ice, arm-in-arm. The house in the distance looked like Amberley Manor, and as Lizzy gazed at the painting trying to take it all in, the magic happened all over again. It was not such a surprise this time, and she admitted it was rather what she'd been hoping would happen all along.

She was standing at the side of the lake, wobbling uncertainly on a pair of ice skates she had no recollection of putting on, when Jane and Elizabeth came skating over. They looked as if they'd just stepped off a Christmas card themselves with their scarlet cloaks and bonnets trimmed with green ribbons, their fur muffs dangling on silk cords and with leather skating boots on their feet.

'I'm so glad you're feeling better!' said Eliza. 'We'd been told you might stay in bed, but I'm glad to see no trifling cold would keep you away.'

Lizzy smiled, but did not know how to answer. She couldn't quite work out how or why she was there. It couldn't possibly be that she was experiencing real time; surely this was yet another doorway into an alternate world she was not familiar with? Jane and Eliza seemed exactly the same, but it was difficult to comprehend just what was happening.

'And I'm glad to see they made room for you in the sleigh,' added Jane. 'I hope it wasn't too noisy with all our cousins. They are so excited to come skating. In London they rarely have a chance, though little Edward tells me he skated on the Thames once when it was frozen over.'

'Your cousins are delightful,' Lizzy added, truthfully. She had no memory of arriving in a horse-drawn sleigh though could see the splendid vehicle behind her, in blue and gold paint, draped with furs and blankets.

'Come, all our friends are here, and there is one who particularly wishes to skate with you,' said Elizabeth.

Lizzy looked questioningly at her friend who only smiled rather mysteriously. She stepped onto the ice, which had the lustre of a Venetian looking glass, sparkling with light from the sun, which hung low in the sky like a scarlet ball. Taking a few tentative steps, and arm-in-arm with Jane and Eliza, the three girls made a charming picture, and were soon skimming over the surface, growing more confident with every stride.

Everyone she knew seemed to be there and enjoying themselves. The little Gardiners skated and tumbled more times than she could count, but were all very jolly for trying to stay on their feet. Kitty skated with one of the officers, Mr Denny, who'd arrived that morning, and Lydia looked very happy on the arm of Mr Wickham. Whether by design or accident, she kept falling into his arms, and every time he prevented her from doing real harm by drawing her closely, she gazed up at him with adoration, laughing as she allowed him to grasp her tightly.

'We really should speak to our sister, Eliza, before she makes a real exhibition of herself,' said Jane.

'I tend to agree; with every partner Lydia's been unable to stand up for more than two seconds together. Though Mr Wickham looks as if he truly enjoys her constant tripping over, I must say.'

'She is behaving outrageously, and needs to be checked. Everyone is looking, and even Mr Darcy looks shocked,' Jane added. 'I've never seen him looking so disapproving.'

'I don't care for his good opinion even if Lydia is being so thoughtless as to behave improperly. Goodness, just look at his expression. She is the silliest girl, but I will not have him be so judgemental. What can he be saying to Mr Williams?'

'Mr Williams is coming over,' said Jane. 'I have a feeling we are about to find out!'

'Good afternoon, ladies.'

Lizzy's mouth almost fell open. She'd watched Mr Williams skate over, bow deeply upon greeting them most cordially, and saw he was now smiling at them. She hardly recognised him without his usual scowl. His smile lit up his features, and added humour to his eyes.

'I wondered if Miss Benson would care to take a turn with me?'

Before she had a chance to answer, he was at her side and proffering his arm. She glanced back at her friends who wore smiles of amusement, and without further hesitation Lizzy took his arm. They skated round the edge of the lake, at first. Neither spoke immediately, as they became used to one another's movements, trying to match their partner as they struck out. Mr Williams matched his strides to hers, taking smaller steps, and the pace of their skating soon settled into a steady rhythm. She leaned on his arm, and once or twice, when she felt herself falter, she felt the firm pressure of his grip, the strong muscles in his arm.

'I hope you are enjoying yourself, Miss Benson, and that you are pleased with Amberley's grounds,' he said, at last.

'I have been here but a short time, but what I have seen pleases me very much,' she answered. 'This is a beautiful lake, and perfect for skating.'

'Thank you, I think this is my favourite time of year, though I wish you could also see its glories in summer. I enjoy boating, and there is nothing like a picnic in the open air.'

Lizzy looked up to examine his countenance more closely. He had all the appearance of Mr Williams, but his smiling manners were so very different, she felt utterly perplexed.

'I should imagine the park and lake would look very beautiful in all seasons.'

'Yes, though of course I am completely biased in my opinion. Amberley is one of the finest houses in the county, unsurpassed except perhaps by Mr Darcy's very own Pemberley.'

'I should not like to choose between them, Mr Williams, and I have not yet had the pleasure of seeing inside Amberley. If it is anything like Pemberley it must be a wonderful house.'

'Mr Darcy speaks highly of Miss Elizabeth Bennet. What is her opinion of Pemberley?'

'I think she admires it. Yes, I am sure she remarked that she did.'

'And what is her opinion of its owner, Mr Darcy?'

Lizzy hesitated. Mr Williams was scrutinising her countenance, and she wondered now if there was a reason for his enquiries. Had Mr Darcy asked him to find out what Eliza thought of him?

'I think she likes him well enough.' Lizzy knew her answer would not satisfy.

'But, perhaps not as highly as he thinks of her. Perhaps she prefers Mr Wickham's company.'

'I cannot tell you.'

Mr Williams didn't speak again for a while, and Lizzy racked her brains for suitable subjects. They made a circuit of the lake once more, and though they were quiet, she felt it was not an uncomfortable silence. Several gentlemen doffed their hats as they glided by, and Lizzy noted others were enjoying themselves on the lake.

Mr and Mrs Bennet were sitting at the side on a bench. Wrapped in blankets and furs, she could see Mrs Bennet talking constantly, whilst her husband closed his eyes against the tirade. One eye opened every now and again, as if he was keeping an eye on the proceedings, but it was very clear he was not listening to a word she said. Mr and Mrs Gardiner were on the ice, making slow but steady progress around the perimeter, and Mr Wickham now had Miss King firmly in his grasp, as they made quite an exhibition with figures of eight.

They were coming round again, and Lizzy noted the same figures still occupied in similar activities, when she saw the figure of a lady she'd not noticed before. As they whirled by she had to turn her head again just to make sure she'd been right, but there was no doubt when the lady in question waved and smiled at her. It was Miss Austen, sitting at her writing desk, and table. She wore a green velvet cloak, a little worn in places, but with a velvet cap of the same hue upon her head topped with a jaunty feather, she made a pretty picture. Her tawny curls cascaded round her face, and she was smiling to herself, with a sort of dreamy expression as if she might be deep in thought. When Lizzy managed to look once more, she saw Miss Austen's head bowed, and busily engaged in writing.

'Did you see Miss Austen?' Mr Williams asked.

'Yes, I did not notice her the first time round.'

'It's a funny thing, but she often appears when we least expect her. Her words and phrases have a wondrous effect on the universe, I find, and leave me quite entranced.'

'Have you read much of Miss Austen's work?' Lizzy asked.

'Oh yes, every word, and I am always in hope that I shall one day be written into her writing. She is a great artist, Miss Benson, but she doesn't know it yet. We must help her find her way. I think you have been of great assistance, but you can do more.'

He was being rather mysterious, Lizzy thought, but she wondered if Mr Williams knew that Miss Austen was having some problems with the plot of the book she was writing.

'I should be very happy to help, but I really feel I am not qualified. I never wrote anything in my life, Mr Williams.'

'But you have read a great deal, my dear, and that is all that counts in this particular instance. You will promise to do what you can?'

Lizzy nodded, as Mr Williams fell silent again and they skated without saying a word for a minute or two. She preferred that they change the subject altogether, especially when she didn't really understand quite what she was expected to do, and questioned his motives for suggesting she interfere in Miss Austen's writing. She was about to speak again when he made a statement which caused her to blush the very same colour as the setting sun, which was sending streams of coral and pink glittering across the scudding clouds.

'I had the most extraordinary dream last night, Miss Benson. I saw you by the bridge yonder.'

Lizzy turned her face away partly to hide her blushes, but also to see the direction in which he was looking. She couldn't see either the bridge or the stream that instantly jumped into her mind, but she had a feeling she knew what he was describing. It must be a place on his estate, she thought, somewhere in the direction he'd indicated with a nod of his head. He didn't utter another word, and when she plucked up the courage to turn round once more, he looked into her eyes with such a knowing expression; she could not hold his gaze.

'Do unexpected people ever creep into your dreams, Miss Benson?'

Lizzy felt her cheeks burn. It was if he could see inside her soul and read her mind.

'No, never,' she whispered, knowing she spoke a lie.

He smiled at her then, and those lips she saw curve enigmatically into a beaming smile, triggered an indescribable feeling of pure pleasure, which felt stronger than any she'd ever experienced before. The sense of longing shocked her. How she wanted him to take her in his arms right then and kiss her. As she stared, she felt bound to him by such a look of pure consciousness that no words seemed necessary. Yet, at the same time as she became aware that their eyes were fixed so completely on the other, fused to the depths of their souls, he started to fade away, little by little, and shrank by degrees into the painting, until the only image she could see was a tiny picture in the calendar of a skating party in the snow.

Chapter 14

Door Number *Fourteen*

It was still morning, she reasoned, and even though Lizzy felt she'd been away for the whole afternoon, and experienced a slice of life elsewhere, she knew that time had not altered. Early morning frost still glazed the panes of glass at her window, and the tiny hole she'd made to peer out of was no larger. There were sounds heralding the day, and when she got up to investigate, down below on the terrace she could see the little Gardiners already up and dressed, and marching out with their nurse for their morning walk.

There was a knock at the door, and cautiously opening it, as she was still not dressed, Lizzy was pleasantly surprised to see Elizabeth standing there.

'Come, Lizzy, we're going to walk to Lambton for some Christmas shopping. Do say you will join us.'

'I would love to, and I promise I will not be long. I am a little late this morning getting up, having slept strangely last night with the oddest dreams, so I could hardly tell if I lived in the real world or in one of my own making.'

'That happens to us all, you know, and will more frequently now Miss Austen is halfway through her editing. You see, she has to think about every likelihood and outcome of each opportunity, and it's my personal belief that she likes to put us through our paces, and make us behave occasionally in ways one would not think possible. It was not a dream, Miss Benson. I hasten to add, you skate rather well.'

'You were there at the lake? Just now, you saw me as I saw you, skating with ...' Lizzy could not say the words.

Elizabeth nodded. 'Yes, I saw you skating with Mr Williams, and I have to tell you that I hope you will not be upset when you see him later and all of that congeniality has disappeared. I expect she was trying him out as a more pleasant character to see what effect he might have on you. I have to say Mr Darcy does not improve as a surly creature. Do you know, he completely ignored me at the lake, and stood at the side refusing to skate with anyone? I am not certain why Miss Austen introduced him at all. To me, he is not a good fit for the story, in either guise.'

Lizzy couldn't think what to say, but was starting to feel mildly annoyed if she was being used as a sort of experiment. So the Mr Williams she'd skated with, the one who had kissed her by the bridge really was a figment of imagination, but not of hers, it seemed. It was becoming clearer that the windows and doors in the calendar were something else entirely. It was a precious gift indeed, she decided, when she stopped feeling cross, and being given a glimpse into the workings of the mind of the great Miss Austen was surely the best possible present, even if it was clear she was always changing her mind about something or other. She would just have to be more on her guard, and not let her emotions be so easily swayed. As for Miss Austen, she really must give her more than a hint that her ideas were not completely going in the right direction.

Lambton was an attractive village, running like a ribbon through the landscape, with a green at its heart, and a good deal of shops along the high street. Lydia and Kitty saw some of the officers as soon as they turned into the main road, and ignoring their sisters' admonitions they ran across the road, narrowly avoiding being struck by a succession of carts and carriages, gigs and coaches.

Jane, Elizabeth, Mary and Lizzy continued into the draper's with the idea of looking at some lace for a present for Mrs Bennet to go with the bottle of lavender water they'd already purchased in Alton. If they all clubbed together, they might be able to manage. Mary was quickly bored and begged to be allowed to visit the circulating library, and so the three left were free to talk to the draper's assistant who pulled out drawers of lace fichus, stoles and veils for bonnets. Some were extremely fine, but Jane soon passed over those as being too expensive, and in the end they were left deciding between a silk lappet edged in lace and a pair of pretty mittens.

They were the only customers in the shop and had the full attention of the assistant, so when the bell on the door clanged behind them they were naturally curious to see who had come in. To their great surprise and astonishment they saw Miss Bingley, the very last person they expected to see. Her countenance was suffused bright pink with consciousness, and it was a moment before anyone spoke, such was the shock of them all.

Jane, as gracious as ever, was the first to speak. 'Miss Bingley, what a delightful surprise to see you; are you staying in Derbyshire?'

'I am, indeed. Mr Darcy has been so very kind as to issue an invitation to Pemberley for the Christmas period, and so here I am.'

Though she did not mention her brother, Elizabeth knew it was highly unlikely she'd be there without him. 'I did not know you were acquainted with Mr Darcy, Miss Bingley. Is your brother here in the vicinity, also?'

'My brother is a great friend of Mr Darcy, and of his sister, Georgiana. Miss Darcy is such an accomplished young lady. I must admit, I did not expect to see *you* here.'

'We are staying at Darley Manor,' said Jane. 'I am so pleased to see you, dear friend.'

Miss Bingley did not return the compliment. 'Oh, Mr Darcy mentioned something about some people employed to look after the house while his uncle is away. Now it all makes sense. That must be some family of yours, I suspect.'

'My Uncle and Aunt Gardiner are looking after the house for their friend, and were kindly invited to bring a house party,' said Elizabeth, noting that Jane was very quiet and had blushed pink. 'We have been enjoying the company of all our neighbours, and hope we shall see you and your brother over the coming days. How long are you staying in Derbyshire?'

'My brother has made no firm plans, but I know as long as Miss Darcy is resident at Pemberley, and has no further plans to remove to London, our stay will be a considerable one. But, I must make haste, and choose a lace fichu for an evening party, which we are attending tonight. My brother and Mr Darcy are waiting for me in the carriage outside, and I do not like to delay them.'

'Please take our place,' said Jane, at last. 'We are not in a hurry.'

Miss Bingley made no further acknowledgement or conversation and bustled to the counter. She spent at least fifteen minutes poring over a dozen different pieces of lace, until declaring that she would have to leave off purchasing any until she could visit the finer warehouses in London. She swept out with barely a nod in their direction. As she opened the door, they could just glimpse the carriage waiting in the street, but there were no sign of the figures inside. When Miss Bingley had gone, Elizabeth and Lizzy saw, all too plainly, how upset Jane was feeling. Her eyes were tinged red, and she was clearly struggling with her composure.

'Come, we can shop another time,' said Elizabeth leading her sister to the door. As they descended the steps, they saw the carriage disappearing round the bend of the road. Taking her sister's arm, Elizabeth patted it reassuringly. 'I have never met anyone so rude in my life before. How dare she imagine that our uncle and aunt have been employed to be housekeepers, and as for her brother's supposed admiration for Miss Darcy, which she took great pains to hint at, I do not believe a word of it.'

'I think I must prepare myself for the truth, Eliza. I know you are trying to be kind, but Miss Bingley was probably just giving me an indication of what is the true position so I will not feel hurt when I find out for certain that he has been courting Georgiana Darcy in London. Perhaps he has plans to marry her.'

'Stuff and nonsense! Mr Bingley is in love with you, Jane, I am certain of that, and so are you in love with him if you examine your heart. She means to put you on your guard, so we will refuse any invitations where you and her brother may be thrown together again. I would not be surprised if her desperate attempts have anything to do with the fact that she is in love with Mr Darcy. If she can convince her brother to be in love with Miss Darcy, her chances with Mr Darcy will be all the greater!'

'Well, it is not likely we will be invited anywhere now,' said Jane. 'If Mr Darcy thinks we are poor retainers I doubt our company will be much wanted in any of the grand houses.'

'Jane, you are not making any sense. I am certain Mr Darcy said nothing of the sort to Miss Bingley. If that were really what he thought, he would not have been so keen to make our acquaintance. Anyway, whatever the case and I am sure I am right, for my own part I couldn't care less if I ever saw him again.'

'And Mr Bingley is quite at liberty to do as he likes,' said Jane. 'I am quite over thinking of him, you know.'

'Be that as it may,' said Elizabeth who glanced at Lizzy, and exchanged a cognisant look, 'if we are invited to Pemberley again, I can assure you we *will* be accepting the invitation!'

For all their brave discussion, the girls were a quiet party on the way home. Jane, especially, was silent and very thoughtful, and the little bursts of conversation which Elizabeth and Lizzy occasionally indulged in to distract her seemed to achieve nothing. When they reached Darley Manor they heard only that Mr Wickham had called in the morning but no invitation had been left. Jane announced that she felt quite relieved, as she didn't think she would be good company, and without saying another word she went upstairs to her room.

'I do not know what to make of this business, Lizzy,' Elizabeth confided. 'Mr Bingley, I am sure, did not know of our being here in the locality, but now it will be difficult when we are thrown together in company.'

'I hope Miss Bingley does not continue to poison her brother against your family, as I am certain she must have, if what she hinted today was true,' Lizzy answered.

'And it may be we will have no way of knowing unless we receive no further invitations out. We will just have to wait and see.'

'I must admit, I am rather looking forward to spending an evening at home without any society,' added Mary who'd been quiet for some time. 'There is something to be said for an evening with a book, and some quiet solitude.'

'Mary, I must say that on this occasion I am in complete agreement!' her sister rejoined.

The girls carried on to the saloon where Mr and Mrs Bennet were sitting opposite Mr and Mrs Gardiner by the side of a cheerful fire. They greeted the girls as if they'd been gone for a week, and Mrs Gardiner bade them sit down to listen to her plans.

'It is high time we entertained,' announced Aunt Gardiner to the general company. 'A small supper party with some dancing would be perfect, and I know Mrs Robinson is very keen to help. We shall invite Mr Wickham with some of his officer friends, Mr Darcy who is so obliging, and Mr Williams who though rather quiet at times, may just need to spend more time in our company to feel at ease.'

'Oh, sister, what a fine thing for my girls, I thank you. There is nothing like dancing for drawing in the young men or for falling in love, that is what I say.'

Elizabeth glanced at Lizzy. 'We shall have to say something about Mr Bingley,' she said quietly to her friend, 'though I do not know what my mother will make of it. And if my aunt does invite Bingley, what will Jane think about that?'

'I think it might be best to say something whilst Jane is not here,' Lizzy replied. 'Your Aunt Gardiner is always very sensible, she will know what is for the best.'

When Lizzy explained that they'd run into Miss Bingley in Lambton, Mrs Bennet's mixed reactions of excitement and composure, curiosity and indifference, were exactly as expected.

'Well, I don't care if we see him or not,' she said, 'and I hope if he tries to court Jane again that she will make him suffer before she smiles too much in his direction. So, he is a friend of that nice Mr Darcy, is he? You would not imagine he would keep such company as young men who go about breaking young girls' hearts.'

'Caroline Bingley was at great pains to point out that Mr Bingley admires Miss Darcy very much,' said Elizabeth. 'It is my belief she only said so much to convince Jane that her brother is courting someone else. I am certain it is only Miss Bingley's scheming that sent him to London in the first place, and though it would cause Jane some pain to see him again, I think it would remind *him* how much he has missed her.'

'In that case, I think we should carry on and send out invitations,' said Mrs Gardiner. 'Mr Bingley will surely know of our presence here by now from Mr Darcy, and we shall soon find out whether or not he means to accept an invitation to Darley Manor. If he does not come, we shall know the reason why, for sure, and if he accepts, then surely Jane has as much chance with Mr Bingley as Miss Darcy or anyone else.'

'Miss Darcy may have a fortune, but my dear Jane is the sweetest girl, and the most beautiful he will ever see. I hope he will consider what he will suffer in not waking up next to the fairest girl in the world for the rest of his life if he chooses another.'

'Mama, he will not be the first young man to marry for money if he does choose Miss Darcy,' said Elizabeth. 'The young men are polite and obliging, but I think we have already seen that those with money are favoured above the rest.'

'You are talking about Mr Wickham, I suppose,' said Mrs Bennet. 'I should not bother about him, if I were you, Eliza, when Mr Darcy seems so keen to pay court.'

'I do not care for a beau or a spouse for myself,' Elizabeth declared, 'but if I can bring my sister back into Mr Bingley's sphere, I am certain he will fall in love with her all over again.'

Jane made an appearance later in the afternoon. She was in better spirits and listened to her aunt's plans with calm composure. Mr Gardiner was calling on all the young men that afternoon and issuing the invitation for the day after tomorrow. The girls were quite looking forward to a quiet evening spent talking and reading, playing cards or entertaining the little Gardiners with drawing and cutting gold paper.

Lizzy went to fetch her book from her chamber after dinner. It was a gothic novel she was enjoying very much, not least because it really gave her goosebumps at night when the old house creaked and groaned, its oak floors and panels reacting to the cold chill at night, or when the wind came moaning through the gaps in the joinery, whistling and sighing as if telling the history of its ages. She picked it up and was just about to leave when the calendar lit up the room once more. Putting down the book and the candle she couldn't resist looking to see what magic lay behind the door. Peeling back the thin card, she found a picture of Amberley Manor, but this time it looked very different to the wintry scene she'd known before. It was a summer's day, the sun high in the sky and the woods and grassy lawns around were lush and green. The picture zoomed a little closer, and she could just make out a carriage arriving before the door, and a reception party waiting for the couple who stepped down amid cheers and applause. It was no ordinary couple, Lizzy could see, but the picture kept her at a distance and she could not make them out. A man and a woman dressed in their finest clothes, the lady in ivory with a lace veil cascading behind her as she took her gentleman's hand. She was certain she could hear applause and cheering, laughter and the sound of church bells pealing from the silver spire close by, ringing out on the summer breeze.

There was no way of knowing the identity of the bride or groom, but the wedding that had clearly taken place was making her feel very strange and really uncomfortable. She couldn't explain why the idea that it was Mr Williams's marriage felt such a strong one or why the thought of that disturbed her so much, but she knew that just for a moment she wanted to cry at the idea that he was marrying someone else.

Chapter 15

Door Number Fifteen

Mr Gardiner told them all at breakfast that his invitations were received with great cordiality and had been accepted by the gentlemen in question, though he had little idea of exactly how many guests would attend. Mr Darcy had indicated that he was sure his house guests would be delighted to come to Darley Manor, but had made no mention of anyone by name. It would remain to be seen whether Mr Bingley would come along with everyone else.

Lizzy felt off colour. She couldn't put her finger on just what it was that was making her feel so despondent, but she couldn't shake off the feeling. After breakfast she put on her cloak, and went out into the garden alone. She needed to have time to herself, and after crossing the terrace she took the path past the shrubbery where she knew it was quieter, and where she was less likely to be disturbed by anyone. At the end of the long avenue of trees, she found a gate, and being unable to resist the view beyond, she opened it, finding herself in an open landscape. Snow was still piled high, covering her boots up to her ankles, the air was very cold, and her breath made puffs of vapour as she walked briskly along, growing quicker in pace with every step. Her mother's advice, of going for a good walk when she needed to have a think, was always good, and she started to feel better as she admired the spectacular scenery. The high peaks in the distance looked majestic, and the wintry pictures on either side were a balm for her soul.

Something was niggling away at her, and she couldn't decide what it was that was upsetting her so much. She didn't question being here in this strange reality any more. Whether she was trapped in an alternate universe, fixed in someone's head, or was just experiencing a dream she could not wake from she couldn't be certain, but she'd given up trying to make sense of it. Her mother knew where she was and she took comfort from that, and all she could hope was that at some stage she might understand, even though she felt that was not likely to be the case. Lizzy couldn't have asked for a more exciting adventure, and she felt that to think about it too much might make it disappear altogether, and take her back to a world she was glad she'd escaped from. Having her heart broken recently, as never before, had taken its toll. Perhaps it had been a mistake to fall in love with her best friend's brother. Lizzy thought about Harry, the image of his too handsome face flashed up in her mind, and she had to stop herself from crying. She'd loved everything about him, and had fallen deeply in love. They'd met at her friend Charlie's house, of course, been thrown together more than ever during the long summer when he was home from university. When he'd first taken her in his arms she thought she might melt with desire, and he'd seemed to love her back just as much. But, what Lizzy hadn't known was that Harry had a girlfriend back there, at Cambridge, and when he'd finally admitted it, she was devastated. She'd sworn never to be so vulnerable again. Lizzy felt the pain of parting from him as if it was yesterday, but it wasn't only losing Harry that had made her feel so miserable. Charlie had offered no sympathy, and no further friendship, taking Harry's side in the whole affair. She and Charlie had always been so close, had shared everything together from their very first day at school, and not to have her in Lizzy's life any more had been an awful blow. Mrs Benson had been very cross about it all, and tried to explain that she was going through a kind of grieving process, saying that when she'd worked it through, she'd be fine, and in the meantime, she'd advised her daughter to go out and meet new friends. Perhaps it was the fact that she felt she and Elizabeth were becoming great friends, that made her feel uneasy, Lizzy wondered. She knew she didn't want anything to upset that friendship, and having it all mixed up with this strange world where time and existence were weirdly familiar and yet completely extraordinary, was complicating matters.

She was not walking long and had hardly resolved any of the thoughts that tumbled round her head, before the muffled sounds of an approaching horse thundering across the snowy fields brought her from her reverie. When she looked up it was a surprise to see that its rider was someone she knew. Mr Williams on horseback was riding full tilt in her direction, but he stopped when he saw her, and raised his hat. He looked very fine sitting on his chestnut stallion. Dressed in deepest navy blue, with a cloak of the same falling in gathers about his shoulders, he had the air of the town about him. Gone were the holly greens and hazelnut browns she'd seen him wearing in the countryside, and there was something in his manner that made her think he was the bearer of bad news.

'Good morning, Miss Benson, I was just on my way up to the house.' He sounded very formal, and she wondered if she'd ever know him well enough to make him smile when he addressed her.

'Good morning, Mr Williams,' Lizzy answered, determined to be friendly even if he couldn't be, and decided he must be teased out of his serious countenance. 'I must say I am surprised to see you ... do you always come by the back gate?'

Was there a hint of a smile at the corner of those lips, she asked herself? Something about the set of his features, the grey eyes that flickered over hers with an intensity she was not expecting made her stomach leap, and set her heart hammering far too loudly. And then he looked away again, and his mouth was sulky and his eyes angry again. He really was a complete nincompoop, she thought, wishing she could use a stronger word, but failing in her courage to do so.

'I have been known to steal up from the garden on occasion, it's by far the quickest way of getting here, as the road winds in and out of the Derbyshire peaks and the journey is twice as long. I am on my way to see Mr Gardiner, though perhaps you could relay a message for me, Miss Benson, as I am in rather a hurry.'

'Of course, I will tell Mr Gardiner straight away. How can I help?'

'I wanted to thank him for his kind invitation, but unfortunately, I will not be able to attend the supper party tomorrow evening, after all. Would you tell him I've been called back to Hampshire.'

Lizzy gazed up at him, and took note of the strong hands, encased in leather, that twitched at the reins keeping his horse in check. He was looking particularly cross, she thought, with an expression she was coming to know rather well. Yet, despite his taciturn looks, she still thought him very good-looking, and felt disappointed that she would not see him the next day at the party, even though she was sure she was mixing up the real person with the fantasy one of those strange dream-like pictures. She must stop imagining him as some sort of romantic hero-type, she thought. He was just bad-tempered and rude, most of the time.

'Will you be gone long?' she managed to say at last.

He shrugged. 'I do not know when I shall return before Christmas, if at all, but it cannot be helped. I am needed there for the time being, and that is all I can say.'

'What can be so important that you must go now?' she asked, but immediately regretted her outburst.

'I cannot discuss the matter. I wish you a good day, Miss Benson.'

Mr Williams raised his hat, and though Lizzy tried to speak, and to engage him further in conversation, he was determined to be gone. He turned tail with a spray of fine snow, and she watched him gallop away in the opposite direction. There was nothing to be done but return home with the message for Mr Gardiner. It was all very mysterious she thought, but then that was typical of Mr Williams. Lizzy decided he was probably just rushing off for some kind of dramatic effect, and didn't believe he could have anything really urgent to have to sort out. He was probably one of those guys who couldn't cope with the competition of the other gentlemen, and in any case, he seemed socially awkward at the best of times. He didn't seem to want to know anyone very well, and having a conversation with him was tortuous for the most part.

She found her way back to the gate, but just as she was closing it behind her, Lizzy happened to catch a glimpse of another figure hurrying away on the opposite side. It was Miss Austen, dressed warmly for the weather in her velvet cloak, a tam o'shanter on her curly head, leather mittens on her ink-stained fingers, and a bundle of papers under her arm. Tapping a feather quill against her chin, she was obviously deep in contemplation. Lizzy wanted to call out, yet knew she would break her train of thought. Wherever she was going now, it seemed plain she'd been writing outdoors, and was thinking about what she would compose next.

When Lizzy went to change for dinner later in the afternoon she made sure she'd given herself enough time to open the calendar, and in her usual way, couldn't wait to find out what she might discover. She climbed the staircase to her chamber, thinking about all that had transpired earlier and couldn't help thinking that despite everyone's remarks she didn't feel quite the same way as they did. Mr Gardiner had received the message earlier with some regret, but no one else seemed to care whether Mr Williams was coming to the party or not. Lydia declared she was glad he was going home because he was always watching her, she said, as if he disapproved of her. Kitty said she felt sorry for those in Hampshire who would suffer his codfish eyes staring at them all day long, and Mrs Bennet agreed that they'd probably all be better off without his surly manners.

When she reached the top, and turned along the corridor to her chamber door, she couldn't help noticing that something was different. It was so very astonishing, that it was a moment before she could decide what to do, but when Lizzy saw the giant-size paper door in place of her own, perforated round the edges like the ones in the calendar, she knew what she must do.

The paper was quite thick, more like stiff card, and after a while she knew pressing alone was not going to be enough. She pummelled and punched, thumped and tore at the door until it gave way, to discover that the light behind it, which poured in sunbeams through the holes was so piercingly bright, that she wondered if she'd stumbled across a room full of angels. When she stepped inside, the light enveloped her like a warm blanket, and the sensation felt so comforting it was as if two strong arms were hugging her tightly. The blinding light was so strong, she couldn't open her eyes, and when she listened, she could hear a voice gently whispering very closely to her ear.

'Follow your heart, and listen to your feelings. Trust your instincts, Lizzy, not first impressions.'

It was impossible to open her eyes. And then she really felt he was by her side, and she caught the fragrance of his cologne, pine needles in a Christmas forest, a hint of spices, and the sharp bitterness of limes. His arms were round her slender form; she felt so close to him she could feel the drum beat of their hearts next to one another. She leaned against his shoulder, and felt his fingers in her hair.

'My darling Lizzy, wait for me,' he said.

Raising her face, she felt the touch of his soft lips, tentatively at first, caressing her own so tenderly that she could only kiss him back with the urgency she was feeling. He drew her nearer still, pecking at her mouth hungrily as if they'd been lovers forever and she responded with such emotion that tears sprang from her eyes and slid to collect in watery pools of happiness at the corners.

And then it was over as quickly as it had started. She opened her eyes with the shock of the sensation. It was cold, and pitch black, now that the light and the warmth of the strong, comforting arms had left her. Lizzy was standing in her chamber, with no fire and no candle, but with the feeling that she was adored like she'd never been before. How she wanted him to come back, and taste those lips and his caresses on her skin once more. Lizzy dared not think or speak his name, for she knew she could never admit that he'd been here in any form or that she'd wanted to return his kiss. All she knew was that she was sorry it was over, and knew in the very depths of her being that she could not deny the feelings he aroused in her.

Chapter 16

Door Number *Sixteen*

When Lizzy woke the following day, the prospect of the day ahead was a welcome distraction from her thoughts of the day before. She rose early, and joined her friends for a hearty breakfast where the conversation revolved around what needed to be done, how they could all help Mrs Robinson, and of course, what gowns were to be worn, and which feathers selected for their hair. The day passed by in a flash, they were so busy. The girls and the young Gardiners were given the task of bringing in some greenery to decorate the mantelpieces in the ballroom, and after tramping through snow, and across the fields they found a selection of spruce fir, holly branches and even some mistletoe growing on one of the apple trees in the orchard. Henry Gardiner, a stout boy of ten, was given the task of dragging it home on a toboggan, and then all the ladies of the house swagged and festooned the woodland treasure with artistic flair. There was a lot of mess, but an enormous amount of laughter, and when everything was done they all declared they'd never seen anything so fine.

With all the preparations, Lizzy hadn't time to check the calendar again until the evening was almost upon her. She was dying to find out what yesterday's painting would show of last night's events, but when she looked there was only a gilded gingerbread heart, beautifully iced with flowers and stars. It was a lovely picture, but not quite what she'd expected to see. Lizzy racked her brains trying to think what it could mean, and decided it probably represented her own heart, deliciously sweet, but easily broken. She was also disappointed to see that the paper door was half-ripped and hanging off, but when she remembered how she'd had to fight her way through it, she supposed it could have been a lot worse.

It took some time to find door sixteen, but at last she found it hidden in a tree. There was no bright light behind it, and she worried about what she might find though she needn't have worried. It was another painting, as detailed and delightfully executed as all the others, depicting a bunch of mistletoe. But this was no ordinary posy; it was what her mother would have called a kissing ball. Suspended on scarlet ribbons the mistletoe had been gathered into a sphere of green leaves and pearl-white berries. Within the ball were real pearls, and twinkling glass decorations, sparkling angels and icicles, feathered birds and red roses, each one individually crafted. It was the most beautiful object she'd ever seen, and Lizzy could see, as it turned, glittering with a radiance of its own that it needed no other illumination as it threw rainbows of spangled light all around her room. It was very pretty, and she couldn't help thinking that the evening to come might hold the promise of pleasure.

When at last she was ready she made her way downstairs, stopping when she saw the bunch of mistletoe strung up in the hall. It wasn't quite the beautiful object in the calendar, but it still made an arresting sight. Lizzy had told her that there would be kisses stolen for every milky berry she could see, and as she looked, there seemed to be a great number.

Jane was looking rather pale, she thought, but Lizzy knew she must be worrying about whether Mr Bingley would make an appearance.

'Eliza,' said Jane, 'you must not fret. We can meet as friends now, I am quite resigned.'

'If you say so,' her sister answered, winking simultaneously at Lizzy. 'Perhaps I will spend all night dancing with him in that case.'

Mr Wickham, Mr Denny, and another officer friend, Mr Chamberlayne, were the first to arrive, followed swiftly by Miss King and her friend, Miss Polesworth. Some of Mrs Gardiner's friends arrived next. Having lived in Lambton in her youth she was delighted to see the Butlers, the Harrisons and the Shawcrofts, and there was a noisy reunion. Last, but by no means least was the Darcy party, which included Mr Darcy, Miss Darcy, and Lady Catherine de Bourgh, and also Mr Bingley and his sister Caroline.

The party was so large that it was not necessary for prolonged conversation as everyone was introduced. Jane and Bingley bowed and curtseyed, both rather cognisant of the other, Lizzy noticed. They had similar complexions, that betrayed every thought passing, and even Mr Bingley's countenance bore the signs of pink blushes. Each one avoided eye contact, though Mr Bingley smiled warmly, and Jane saw that he was being as friendly as possible.

Mrs Gardiner had thought everything out very carefully. It was to be a buffet supper, with little tables scattered round the dining room, which meant everyone could stick to their own company if they wished, and apart from the Gardiners who moved around to speak to all their guests the little groups stuck to those they'd arrived with, by and large. By the time supper was eaten, and several glasses of wine consumed, everyone seemed in great good humour and ready for some dancing.

The ballroom looked magnificent, and the orchestra started playing as they entered the room. Lizzy watched Mr Darcy ask Jane for the first dance, Mr Bingley approached Elizabeth, and she was surprised to be asked by one of Mrs Gardiner's friends, Mr Shawcroft, a young man about her own age. Mr Wickham was partnering Mary King, of course, and Miss Bingley who looked as if she might be left sitting down for a moment, was asked by Mr Harrison, the eldest of the young men in that family.

The first dance went off very well, but Lizzy was not really concentrating on the steps or her partner. She was too busy in observing everyone else, and was not surprised to see how often Mr Bingley looked at Jane. Miss Bennet hardly looked up from the floor, except to answer Mr Darcy when he spoke to her, and when she accepted her next dance with Mr Butler, a particularly good friend of Mrs Gardiner, Lizzy saw that Mr Bingley looked fit to burst. Jane was so much in demand from all the young gentlemen that Mr Bingley could not get a look in, and when the time came for a break in the proceedings and for the dancers to catch their breath, he could not get anywhere near her she was so completely surrounded by eager young bucks.

Mrs Bennet was delighted. 'Mr Bingley must be regretting that he did not take his chance earlier,' she said, with a purse of her lips. 'Oh, Jane, I hope you will keep him dangling, my dear, and that you will not give in too soon. He needs a lesson learned, that one.'

Jane was not in the vicinity when she spoke these words, and though Lizzy was sure Jane would never behave accordingly, she was pleased to see that Mr Bingley was looking on anxiously, uncertain what to do next. Lizzy knew there would be other occasions, and even if they didn't get a chance to dance tonight, there was hope for another time.

'I could not have asked for a better start to this evening,' Elizabeth confided in her. 'Bingley is beside himself. He clearly hadn't the wherewithal to ask Jane for the first dance, which is why he got Mr Darcy to do it, but he must be sorry now. Jane's card is full, I am certain.'

'Yes, it may not really be the outcome Jane would wish for, but I think it will be better to make him wait,' Lizzy answered. 'And it's all great fun to watch!'

'Look, Jane is dancing with that handsome Mr Harrison next. Poor Mr Bingley is forced to dance with his own sister.'

'Miss Bingley seems most put out,' agreed Lizzy, 'she hasn't once yet succeeded with Mr Darcy, and for all her efforts to throw Miss Darcy in his way, she has accomplished nothing. They had a dance near the start, but he hasn't asked her again.'

'Has Mr Darcy asked you for a dance, Elizabeth?' asked Lizzy.

'No, thank goodness,' she replied, though Lizzy wasn't entirely convinced by her answer. She hoped he was giving her a little of the treatment she generally bestowed upon him. Ignoring her might be the very thing to help him succeed.

'Don't you think he looks rather cross this evening?' said Elizabeth, casting a glance at him. 'Just look at his countenance; he really is a very strange man. One minute he's all smiling affability, the next he's a crabbed, and disapproving spoilsport. I really cannot make him out.'

Lizzy looked across the room. Mr Darcy certainly looked rather bad-tempered, though she didn't think that had been his general demeanour of the evening. She followed his gaze, and saw him frown even more. The people he seemed to be watching with such distaste were Mr Wickham and Lydia Bennet. The latter was pulling on Mr Wickham's sleeve, and laughing rather brightly and perhaps a little loudly. Her companion was whispering something in her ear, which set Lydia off into peals of snorting laughter. Looking back to Mr Darcy, Lizzy noted he was looking on most disapprovingly, and when she suggested to Elizabeth that might be the cause, she nodded in agreement.

'I see what you mean, I really must speak to her, but I do not see why Mr Darcy should be troubling himself about it. He really is turning into a prig, in my opinion. Whatever I think about his behaviour, I do not go around looking down my nose at him. I daresay Miss Bingley has been telling him how poor we really are, and that is why he has not asked me to dance.'

Lizzy did not know how to answer this tirade, and fortunately did not have to as their partners for the next dance arrived at their side to whisk them away.

The evening was deemed a great success by Mrs Gardiner and Mrs Bennet, though Lizzy seemed peevish, and Jane rather quiet by the end of it. Lydia and Kitty were the only two who really seemed in good spirits, and as they were all discussing the events, the former came to sit next to Lizzy to ask her how she did, and whisper in her ear.

'I have a great secret,' she said, 'and you must promise not to say a word.'

Lizzy smiled encouragingly; she was used to Lydia's foolishness, which usually didn't amount to much. 'Cross my heart,' she answered.

From her reticule, Lydia brought forth a sprig of mistletoe. 'See this, Miss Benson? It had four berries on it.'

Lizzy didn't catch her meaning straight away, but when she did, and Lydia saw that she'd understood, she couldn't help feeling on her guard.

'Lydia, I do not think I want to know any more, but I will say this. It's not a good idea to go around kissing people on a whim, especially gentlemen you don't know well, even if it is nearly Christmas.'

'Oh, do not be silly, I know the gentleman in question perfectly well!' She giggled and looked conspiratorially round the room before whispering once more. 'It's not the first time he's kissed me - I declare he is in love with me, though I am not certain of my full regard. Promise you won't say a word?'

Lizzy was only slightly mollified by the fact that Lydia had not fallen for this rogue, hook, line and sinker, but did not feel comfortable keeping such a secret or hearing it had happened before.

'I won't say anything on this occasion, Lydia, but I will not promise to do so if I hear you do such a thing another time. Think what would happen if you were found out, or if this gentleman pressed his attentions on you further. You know it is not right.'

'No, but I simply love it, and if I could be kissed everyday in such a way, I would be in heaven, indeed!'

There was nothing more Lizzy could say, and she could only ponder on how it was possible that she felt so able to offer such pertinent advice when she was the very person who needed a good dressing down having indulged in exactly the same activity. Kissing Mr Williams, whether a figment of her imagination or the real person, and more than once, had been as foolhardy as any kissing Lydia had done. But like her foolish friend, she knew if she had the chance, she'd probably do exactly the same again.

Chapter 17

Door Number *Seventeen*

Lizzy was already awake when she heard sounds outside the door, as if someone might be about to knock and were dithering in their decision to do so. She'd been lying there for some time thinking about Mr Williams who she'd missed yesterday, despite telling herself many times that she just wasn't bothered about the fact that he was no longer around to scowl at her. Whenever she tried to analyse her feelings about him, she couldn't, and it was impossible to fathom out exactly why she felt such an attraction to him. He was really good-looking, of course, but he didn't endear himself to anyone on any other level. The only conversations she'd had with him where he seemed to be anything like a normal human being were on occasions when reality and her dreams had been fused, and more than once, it occurred to her that this wasn't a true reflection of his personality.

There were still scuffling noises to be heard beyond the door, and as she looked over she saw something being pushed under the door. On investigation it proved to be a note written on stiff cream paper.

Dear Miss Benson,

Forgive me for this call upon your time but I cannot wait any longer - I am afraid it is imperative that we speak again. Please join me in the library as soon as you can.

Yours ever,

Miss J. Austen.

The note sounded rather urgent, so Lizzy jumped out of bed and got dressed as quickly as she could. It was still very early, and only the maids and servants could be heard going about their daily business. Footsteps running up and down the wooden staircases, the clank of pails, the swishing of a sweeping broom, and the early smells of bacon frying alerted her senses to the fact that she was not the only person up and ready for the day.

Lizzy hadn't ventured into the library before and when she pushed open the door, it was to discover a wonderful room with book-lined shelves. She couldn't think at first why the vast libraries she'd visited in other grand houses with her parents had never felt they were rooms in which to linger, when it struck her that they always seemed rather impersonal, comfortless and cold. Those other libraries had looked like mere collections of books to impress people, but this room was different. For a start there was a roaring fire in the grate sending flames licking up the chimney like the golden antlers of a stag, and so many candles set in candelabras or in sconces on the walls and in porcelain candlesticks studded with flowers that the room glowed with flickering halos throwing bars of honey beams like splashes of toffee-coloured paint onto every surface. There were books open on the tables set about to encourage the readers to pick them up, and piles of books next to every chair arranged on small tables so it was easy to put out a hand and pick one up. It was simply her idea of heaven. And there, in the midst of it all, was Miss Austen seated at her own little table with its many sides, her writing desk atop and scattered all over with pieces of paper, a bottle of ink, and a rather short quill, which had clearly seen much use.

She rose when she saw Lizzy, and the little frown that was crossing her brow when Lizzy first walked in lifted and disappeared entirely. Her smile lit up her face. 'Come in and join me, Miss Benson - I'm so glad you could come. I'm working myself into ill humour, and I cannot decide what to do.'

'Well, I hope I can help you,' said Lizzy feeling completely inadequate, knowing that she was speaking to the greatest writer who ever lived.

'Tell me, am I right to keep Jane and Bingley apart for so long?' Miss Austen began. 'It seems cruel to go on giving the poor girl little hope of a reconciliation, and yet, this is what happens in real life, as I know to my cost.'

Lizzy couldn't decide whether Miss Austen was referring to *Pride and Prejudice*, which she knew well, or whether she was making some sort of reference to what was happening now. And what did she mean about her own few hopes of reconciliation?

'I suppose keeping them apart makes the reader want to know what happens next,' answered Lizzy, 'and it creates tension and drama. I think everyone likes a little suffering for their heroines before finding a happy ending.'

'A happy ending isn't always the outcome for true heroines, Miss Benson. In real life they are hardly ever found. As a writer of novels, isn't it my purpose to present a world that my readers recognise and can understand. Shouldn't my books reflect the world in which we live?'

'I think they should, and your genius is in doing exactly that, in your observations of people, and in the delineation of their characters. Your novels truly act as a mirror of the society in which we live. You are such a genius that people two hundred years from now will still recognise your Elizabeth Bennet, Emma Woodhouse, and Anne Elliot, but you have never been one to dwell on guilt and misery.'

'No, that is true enough. I may be guilty of many things, and have been miserable on many an occasion, but I always make it a rule to put those dilemmas behind me and look to brighter days and sunnier thoughts. I certainly do not want my books to be full of gloom. But, Emma Woodhouse and Anne Elliot are not names with which I am familiar, Miss Benson. Do enlighten me.'

'Oh, they really aren't worth worrying about at present,' Lizzy replied, suddenly remembering that they'd not been imagined or written about yet, but I do urge you to write a happy ending, even if the journey that gets them there is ever so slightly fraught along the way.'

'Yes, I suppose you are right, and I must admit, though I did enjoy making him suffer yesterday, I know I will not be able to keep it up. He does love her, and she loves him ... they are so well suited in so many ways. She is my dear sister to the life.'

'I wondered if she might be.'

'Tell me, what do you think of Mr Darcy? How is *he* shaping up?'

'When I first met him, I must admit I was a little confused by his manners, but last night I caught a glimpse of the Mr Darcy I know so well.'

'I knew it! I was right to tinker with him! There's a certain phrase that keeps going round in my head, Miss Benson. You do not have to be specific, but just indicate if it is known to you. *One has got all the goodness, and the other all the appearance of it.* I cannot get it out of my head, and I think it may be the key.'

Lizzy couldn't help smiling. 'Oh, Miss Austen, I implore you to listen to those thoughts. You are really onto something now, and I believe you are about to resolve every question.'

'I do not need to know any more, Miss Benson, but I thank you. Together we are finding the path, and we'll march on to the end. I rather like my dour Mr Darcy, and his vexing my delightful Elizabeth is pure joy to write. Well, we shall see what happens next. I know this may not be the last draft, but we're certainly making progress. You may go about your business, my dear, and thank you, once again.'

Lizzy got up to go rather hesitantly. She wanted to ask Miss Austen a question, but she didn't dare. She was almost at the door when she turned. Jane saw her expression, noted the biting of her lip.

'Is there something I can help you with?' she asked.

'Mr Williams has gone back to Hampshire,' Lizzy said. 'Do you know if he'll be back before Christmas?'

'That is a question I cannot answer, my dear,' said Jane, 'we will just have to wait and see.'

Lizzy said goodbye and let herself out, closing the door behind her. There was no reason why Miss Austen would know his plans or why Mr Williams had gone back, she supposed, but she'd answered with such an air of mystery Lizzy couldn't help wondering if Jane knew more than she was letting on. If only she could stop thinking about him, she was sure she'd be much happier. She was positive he wasn't wasting endless hours thinking about her, and it annoyed her that he'd got so under her skin. She didn't even like him, and she was sure her mother would think he was the rudest man she'd ever met. Though why she was daydreaming about the possibility of his meeting her mother, she didn't want to question.

When she reached her chamber, she tried to resist opening the door of number seventeen. She was sure she'd find nothing she wanted to see, and she picked up her book to take with her to read downstairs until everyone else joined her for breakfast. Everywhere suddenly seemed so quiet in the room it made her ears ring. All the familiar sounds were gone, and when she looked outside there was not a soul to be seen. And then she heard horse's hooves, thudding on the snow, the sound growing louder until she was sure the horse must be below her window though when she looked through the window once more, there were no steed or rider anywhere in sight. But the sound wasn't coming from the window, she decided, and it didn't take long for her to reason from where the clopping noises came. The calendar door was lit up, brighter than ever, pulsating with the beams of light. It was bulging, and popping out of shape as if something behind it was trying to force its way out. The noise was deafening, as if an army on horseback were about to storm into the room. Lizzy pulled at the perforations, but before she'd managed to work her way round, a miniature horse complete with rider burst out and galloped across the top of the chest of drawers. She was so surprised, and felt so frightened that she dropped the calendar, leapt back on the bed, and could only watch as the horse and its gentleman rider jumped down, almost in a flying action to gallop round the room, and back again, jumping up from whence they came.

When she plucked up the courage to pick it up again, and look at the calendar, there was only the usual painting to see. She recognised Chawton cottage in the snow, and the horse that had just galloped around her room. As for the gentleman who was riding it, he had his back to her, but she knew perfectly well that she recognised him, and when he suddenly sprang into life again, as he led his horse to the barn, she called out his name. Mr Williams didn't turn or wave, but simply turned his horse away.

Chapter 18

Door Number *Eighteen*

There was always great excitement when the letters arrived in the morning. Mrs Bennet received a great deal of news and gossip from her sister Mrs Phillips who lived in Alton, Mrs Gardiner often heard from her friends in London, and the girls always waited in high expectation of invitations. On this particular morning, Mrs Bennet and Mrs Gardiner both received the kind of letters they'd been waiting for, and Mr Darcy's invitation for the following evening promised a ball. There would be dancing, cards and supper, which they all looked forward to with great anticipation.

Lizzy didn't expect to receive any post. Neither her mother or sister Lily were usually great letter writers preferring to text her if they needed to send a message when she was away from home, so she was surprised to see a letter in her mother's hand. Still, as her phone had run out of battery a long time ago she supposed it was the one line of communication left to them, and felt rather ashamed that she hadn't taken any steps towards writing a letter herself. Still, she couldn't help feeling a certain trepidation as she opened it, imagining that it must be something urgent to make her mother put pen to paper.

Dear Lizzy,

I hope you're having a lovely time - we've been very quiet since you've been gone, and even more so because your sister is hardly ever at home these days. What a thing it is to be young - make the most of it, I say, you've got plenty of time to be old, and I know - :)

Do you remember that boy, George, Lily has always liked? They've been seeing one another on and off, though I'm not quite sure about it because I bumped into Penelope Harrington the other day, and she said she thought he was engaged. Anyway, I can never get two seconds to talk to Lily about it, she's always out, and now she says she's going to stay with friends in Brighton for Christmas, and not spend it with your Dad and me. It's impossible to reason with her, but I was just the same at sixteen, and she'll grow out of it - I hope! Have you heard from her lately? I'm not sure what I should do about it, but her friend Harriet is a nice girl I remember, though I've only met her once, and her father is something high up in the army, so I'm sure she'll be okay. If you do hear something, would you let me know, dear?

I had a nice letter from that Mr Williams on the 14th - isn't he charming? He writes quite formally, and signs himself, D. Williams, no first names or anything like that, but I suppose that's his upbringing being as he was educated at boarding school, he told me. But there's nothing wrong with old-fashioned manners, I always say, and he wrote to tell me you were well, and enjoying yourself. He mentioned you were a particularly good skater - fancy that, I thought, I couldn't remember you ever going skating in your life before. He said he was going back to Hampshire on business soon, and was very sorry about it because he'd been having a lot of fun with you all at Darley Manor. He does sound like a nice boy, so I hope you don't mind, but I wrote back and we've exchanged another letter since. He loved the photo I popped in the envelope of you and Lily when you're about six, and she's just a toddler - you know the one - it's so cute. It was taken one Christmas and you didn't want to smile because you'd just lost both of your front teeth. I expect he's gone back to Chawton by now, and you're probably missing him.

Anyway, I just thought I'd send a note to keep in touch. Mr Williams seemed to think you wouldn't be back until after Christmas so we'll celebrate altogether when you come home.

Hope to hear from you soon!

Love Mum xxx

Lizzy read the letter through three times and still could not believe the words she saw dancing in front of her eyes. Never mind that Lily was being completely thoughtless and clearly badly behaved as usual, her mother had been swapping letters with Mr Williams, of all people, and it seemed they'd exchanged a fair bit of information in what could only have been a matter of days. She'd been sending him photos and telling him tales, by the sounds of things, and Lizzy could just imagine what a laugh he must have enjoyed at her expense, egging her mother on as if he was Lizzy's best friend. How she hated him at that moment. The very thought of it made her feel so angry that she was glad she couldn't speak to her mum on the phone, for she knew she'd have given her a piece of her mind, and the shame of thinking about all that might have been said, caused her to blush beetroot red. Her hands were shaking she was so cross, and when Elizabeth asked her if anything was the matter she was forced to quickly pull herself together. She didn't want to share any part of the letter, and quickly replied that everything was just fine, and that she'd just been thinking of home.

'Miss Benson, I believe we've been very selfish making you come away with us all for so long,' said Elizabeth. 'You were bound to miss your family.'

'Oh, Miss Elizabeth, please do not worry, I am quite content. I shall very soon be spending as much time as I like in their company, and I assure you, that although I love them dearly, I am not in a hurry to go home.'

'And, if you were to go home now you would miss the ball tomorrow!'

'Yes, I am looking forward to it very much.'

Elizabeth turned to her sister Jane to ask her which gown she was to wear for the ball, and Lizzy was left to her own thoughts once more. She couldn't help thinking about the letter again, and a thought struck her that she'd not considered before. Mr Williams had told her mother about the skating, which meant he had a remembrance of it, and when she examined the memories of that day she blushed even more. He'd talked of his dreams and had asked her if she ever dreamed of people she knew. She'd lied because of the kiss they'd shared by the bridge, and now she couldn't help thinking that he'd known perfectly well that the kiss had been as real for him as it had for her. The idea made her experience a strange excitement, and as much as she tried she could not entirely work out why.

There was no need to look inside the calendar when she went upstairs to look at it later, she knew the subject of today's painting would be a letter or series of letters. But Lizzy could never leave one of the doors without opening it. She was quite right. The painting showed a dear little robin with a scarlet breast and the letter in his beak; a sprig of holly in the corner completed the festive theme along with a sprinkling of silver glitter. He set it down and chirped when he saw Lizzy, a heavenly birdsong that had the effect of dispelling any gloomy thoughts. She was rather comforted by it, and on taking out her mother's letter again, read it with renewed interest.

Chapter 19

Door Number *Nineteen*

Christmas had arrived at Pemberley. A yule log burned in the great hall, which was decked in greenery, and everywhere looked festive with fir, holly and ivy decorating every surface. Lizzy had never seen so many people in her life, and if Mr Darcy's parties had been well attended before, now it seemed as if the entire neighbourhood were arrived at his door. The gowns of the ladies were sumptuous, everyone dressed in their finest for what was the ball of the season.

'Pemberley always brings together the best company in the land,' Lizzy heard Lady Catherine bragging to a lady and her husband who looked too intimidated to move away. 'My nephew has taken up where his dear parents left off, and I can assure you, there will not be another ball of this magnitude held in the county until he gives the word to repeat it this time next year. Of course, when Sir Lewis de Bourgh was alive, we delighted our neighbourhood with seasonal hospitality, but now my nephew insists on my being here to help him, and stand in his mother's place, Rosings must remain quiet. It is a pity but, I ask you, who am I to disoblige him?'

Lizzy didn't think Mr Darcy seemed to be relying on his aunt quite as much as that lady was making out. He seemed rather distracted this evening, she thought, and whilst not exactly unwelcoming, he'd barely exchanged more than two words with any of their party when they were received, and he'd completely ignored Elizabeth when she'd declared how much she was looking forward to the dancing. What was more, he'd not asked her for a single dance, and Lizzy could tell, though she protested against it, that Eliza was rather put out.

Mr Bingley, on the other hand, was charming and talkative, and made his way over to join them as soon as he could, his sister Caroline following in his wake. She looked as cross as Mr Darcy, and was clearly having trouble arranging her features so as not to betray her true feelings when her brother asked Jane for the first two dances.

Lizzy and Elizabeth, who were standing next to Jane when Mr Bingley announced his offer, immediately took the other's hand, squeezing them hard in excitement. Jane looked as composed as ever, though what she was truly feeling Lizzy did not like to speculate. But, when she smiled, she exuded happiness, which was wonderful to see.

'Thank Mr Bingley for his kind offer, Jane,' said Mrs Bennet. 'We are so delighted to see you, sir. It's high time you danced together again, we couldn't think what you were waiting for!'

'Mama,' said Elizabeth, taking her mother's arm, and leading her away, 'come let us find a seat so we can watch the proceedings.'

Lizzy followed, trying not to chuckle. Mrs Bennet really knew how to put her foot in it!

The dancing soon started in earnest, and Lizzy was happy to stand up with some of the young men she'd met at Darley Manor. Mr Butler, and Mr Harrison allowed themselves to be abused by Elizabeth's teasing, and they made good partners, dancing twice with each of them, but it was noted by Lizzy that Mr Wickham and Mr Darcy kept well away, not even coming over to converse. Mr Darcy did not dance at all. He barely spoke to anyone, and looked about him as if he wished to be anywhere else. His manner was so changed that he almost appeared to be a different person. Occasionally,

Lizzy saw him staring at Eliza; especially when she was dancing or making Mr Butler laugh, but his expression was so impassive she could not make out what he was thinking.

'What on earth is the matter with Mr Darcy?' said Elizabeth at last.

Lizzy looked at her friend's countenance, and couldn't help thinking she looked nearly as angry as their host, who was not being attentive or ensuring that his guests were being entertained.

'The only person who seems to have his interest is Caroline Bingley,' said Lizzy, 'though he's hardly spoken to her, despite all her efforts to engage him in conversation.'

'I noticed that,' answered Elizabeth, 'she must be so frustrated. She has stood next to him for a full half hour now, and not once has he asked her to dance.'

'No, but he is not dancing with anyone.'

'I always thought him disagreeable, but at least his manners formerly were congenial. I have found him out at last and discovered him to be proud, to be above his company, and rude. It was all an act, I find, and in this case my first impressions were not wrong. I could never quite trust him. People who are truly unpleasant cannot keep up a pretence of that sort forever. Look at him now; his surly expression would turn good milk sour!'

Lizzy didn't think he looked particularly surly, but he didn't look happy, and despite Elizabeth's exclamations, she noted how often her companion looked over at him, even when she declared she was not interested in him. He was busy observing Eliza covertly also, and Lizzy wished she could think of a way to bring them together. All this tension between them was highly charged, and she believed that if only she could arrange for them to come together everything might fall into place.

Mrs Bennet was beside herself with happiness. Jane and Bingley had danced together three times, and now stood apart from everyone else deep in conversation.

'I think we'll see a wedding at last,' she said, tapping her fan on Mrs Gardiner's arm. 'I knew he could not keep away, and Jane did so well to keep him at arm's length last time. She is so beautiful and he cannot resist her. Well, he had better make his plans known soon if he is to keep her, because there is a queue of gentlemen waiting to take his place if he does not.'

Mrs Gardiner smiled. 'I am sure you are right, sister. I never saw a couple so well suited, and I am certain he would not be paying her such attention if his intent was not serious this time.'

'At least I will have one girl off my hands. It vexes me to think that Eliza has passed over so many opportunities to walk down the aisle. But, I've never been able to make her see sense, and she is so headstrong. First there was Mr Collins, and then Mr Wickham paid her court, but neither were good enough, it seems. That nice Mr Darcy seemed to prefer her above everyone else when we first came to Derbyshire, and now he will not even speak to her, let alone dance with her. He's given up, that's plain to see.'

'You should not worry so much, dear,' Mrs Gardiner replied. 'I am sure Elizabeth's knowing her own mind will stand her in good stead in the long run. She is very discriminating, and I'm sure we neither of us would wish her an alliance, which would not suit.'

'If you mean by that she is very choosy, I will agree, but I am convinced she will end up an old maid! What will become of us all?'

Mrs Gardiner chose not to answer, and Mrs Bennet attempted to lift her thoughts with more cheerful contemplation by watching her eldest daughter and making wedding plans.

Supper was a noisy affair. The vast dining room was filled with tables, and the hungry dancers set about demolishing the Christmas fayre with relish. There were turkeys by the dozen, roasted and carved upon silver platters, with dishes of cold ham, and dressed salmon, tureens of white soup, plates of pink lobsters and haunches of beef, all to be washed down with the finest wines brought up from Pemberley's cellars. It amused Lizzy to see the company, particularly the gentlemen, become louder and less refined as consumption increased. But she also knew that Elizabeth was becoming increasingly disturbed by Lydia and Kitty's behaviour. Lydia, it seemed, had been given a glass or two of punch by one of Mr Wickham's friends, and she was becoming rather loud and drawing much attention to herself. Once or twice, Lizzy saw her looking at Mr Wickham himself with admiring eyes, and she couldn't help feeling perturbed by it. She didn't want to alarm Elizabeth further, so kept her thoughts to herself; deciding to keep an eye on Lydia. There had never been any particular preference for his company before, she was sure, and after all, Mr Wickham was not the man she'd imagined he would be. He was a gentleman, and everybody spoke of his good character.

After supper, some of the ladies performed upon the pianoforte, and Elizabeth was called upon. The whole room seemed enraptured by her playing, and none more so than Mr Darcy whose eyes never left her. Elizabeth was looking very beautiful, Lizzy thought. She was dressed in white, in a simple style, her high waist cinched in with a wide sash, which made her womanly figure appear to great advantage. With her dark curls piled high on her head, those that had escaped trembled on her nape. Her slender, white arms moved over the keyboard, her fingers flying as she played a collection of favourites. Mr Darcy was entranced. Lizzy saw his eyes linger on her lovely face before they dropped to the slope of her breasts where a lace fichu was fastened with a silk flower. He was completely besotted, Lizzy realised, and she wondered if his reluctance to dance had anything to do with the fact that far from being rude, he was simply overawed by Elizabeth, and felt out of his depth.

The evening was passing at a pace, and the dancers called back to the ballroom. As they rushed to find their seats, Lizzy heard Mr Darcy's voice behind them.

'Miss Bennet, may I speak with you.'

Elizabeth turned, but didn't answer. He hesitated before speaking again, and although he still bore that same taciturn expression, his voice was softer than before. 'Will you dance with me?'

Her answer came swiftly, and no sooner had she agreed than she turned angrily to her friend when he was out of earshot. 'Why did I agree to dance with him? I cannot abide him, and now I will have to talk to him.'

'Eliza, have you considered that he may be in love with you, and that he's been struggling with his feelings? I must admit, I've been observing him all evening, and he's hardly taken his eyes off you.'

'Mr Darcy in love with me? I fear your teasing has gone too far this time, Miss Benson.'

'No, I assure you, I would not do such a thing. Perhaps you should give him a chance; you may have more in common than you think, and he is a good dancer, you can't deny that.'

'I am not giving him an inch, but I will be kind to him for your sake, and will allow him five minutes before I abuse him to his face. As for his dancing, I will say he has a fine leg, and performs in a cotillion with grace and verve when he deigns to join in.'

Lizzy laughed. 'Be gentle, I think he has a genuine regard for you, and I have a feeling he will shape up to be a very gentleman-like character before too long.'

'I cannot share your optimism, dear friend, but for your sake, I shall try my very best on this one occasion.'

When the ball was over, the weary party that left for Darley Hall were all agreed that they'd enjoyed themselves immensely. Jane was quiet, but exuded pure happiness, Lydia and Kitty talked endlessly of their partners, and Elizabeth went so far as to admit privately to Lizzy that she'd enjoyed dancing with Mr Darcy to a certain extent.

There was a moment, as Lizzy got ready for bed, when she decided she would leave the calendar and open it the next day. But when she got into bed, the light pouring from the perforations was so intense she knew there was nothing else to be done. She'd spent most of the evening being successful in not thinking about the one person who'd been unable to attend. Now, as she peeled back the door he came into her head, and she couldn't help thinking about Mr Williams or what he was doing right now. The picture gave her a little start when she saw it was a kissing couple, and with mounting excitement wished she could be drawn instantly into the painting.

To her great disappointment, nothing happened. And when she peered closer, she saw it was not an image of the gentleman she was hoping for, and the young lady who was kissing him back was certainly not a depiction of herself. The painting loomed larger, and with the realisation of just whom the couple represented, she gasped out loud, putting her hand to her mouth in shock. A sleepless night was looming before her, and all she could think about was how soon she could tell Elizabeth of her suspicions, and to be on her guard.

Chapter 20

Door Number *Twenty*

The moment Lizzy awoke next morning she knew something was not right. It seemed she'd overslept, for she could hear all the family already below, and making rather a lot of noise, which was unusual in itself at so early an hour. She listened intently, and soon heard that sometimes the voices were raised in anger, mostly from one particular person whose piercing tones were now quite familiar. She didn't want to be any later than necessary so pulling her clothes on quickly, and splashing a little water on her face, she assembled her hair into a makeshift knot on the top of her head before running downstairs to see what was going on. She hadn't quite entered the breakfast parlour when she heard Mrs Bennet screeching at the top of her voice.

'Oh, my poor Lydia! What can have happened to her, and why was she persuaded to do such a thing? Kitty, you are as much to blame for her behaviour ... how could you have kept their going away a secret until this morning?'

When Lizzy entered the room, she saw Kitty standing before her mother's chair, red in the face, and with tears running down her cheeks. 'I knew nothing of her plans, Mama! That is most unfair - I told you as soon as I found the letter, and all you can do is blame me. It is not my fault!'

Mrs Bennet flopped further into her chair in an attitude of despair, whilst Mr Bennet looked on quite aghast, though completely ineffectual having not quite managed to put down his newspaper. Elizabeth and Jane, looking most distressed, were seated on either side of their aunt and uncle who were holding their hands and speaking to them both in a reassuring manner, as Mary looked from one to the other, and over the top of her glasses perched on the end of her nose with such an expression of horror that it was clear she'd been left quite speechless.

'Read the letter to me again, Kitty, and speak up this time!' Mrs Bennet commanded.

Kitty unfolded the letter with shaking hands and read.

MY DEAR KITTY,
You will laugh when you know where I am gone, and I cannot help laughing myself at your surprise tomorrow morning, as soon as I am missed. I am going to Brighton, and if you cannot guess with whom, I shall think you a simpleton, for there is but one man in the world I love, and he is an angel. I should never be happy without him, so think it no harm to be off. You need not tell them straight away at Darley Manor of my going, if you do not like it, for it will make the surprise the greater, when I write to them and sign my name, Lydia Wickham. What a good joke it will be! I can hardly write for laughing. Mr Wickham says we can get a special licence to marry in Brighton and I cannot wait. What do you think, Kitty? Is this not the most exciting adventure I've had yet?

I shall send for my clothes as soon as I can; but I wish you would tell Sally when you get home to mend a great slit in my worked muslin gown before they are packed up. Goodbye. Give my love to Captain Denny. I hope you will drink to our good journey.

Your affectionate sister, LYDIA.

Mrs Bennet wailed again, louder than ever. 'I always knew he was not to be trusted. Too good-looking and simpering by half! And now he's taken off my dearest girl, and I know he cannot mean to marry her. Brighton is not Gretna Green, there will be no special licence and my Lydia shall be ruined. Mr Bennet, what are you waiting for? You and my brother must find them before it is too late.'

Mr Bennet put down his newspaper and looked to his brother-in-law who agreed there was not a moment to delay. 'And you must make arrangements to return to Chawton, my dear. If Mr Gardiner leaves for Brighton in his coach, you must take ours.'

'Oh dear, yes - I shall feel better if I am at home, and it will not be so far from Brighton for Lydia to come home again.' Mrs Bennet dissolved into racking sobs at this exclamation, and could not be consoled. Mr Bennet and Mr Gardiner left the room in haste, and were immediately heard shouting to the servants to get the carriages ready and to prepare their luggage.

In the midst of all this confusion, the arrival of two gentlemen on horseback, seen cantering through the long windows prompted another outburst from Mrs Bennet.

'And now here is Mr Bingley and Mr Darcy come to propose to you girls, and when they find out what has happened they'll drop you both quicker than hot potatoes. Oh, what is to become of us?'

'Come, Mama,' urged Kitty, drying her eyes with a sodden hankerchief, 'I think it best if you go to your room. Jane and Elizabeth will speak to the gentlemen. Perhaps they know nothing of the business.'

'And even if they do not, how long will it be before they do? Foolish girl, keep quiet unless you can have a rational thought in your head,' Mrs Bennet snapped, 'I will never forgive you, Kitty, as long as I live. You know your sister, and you should have taken better care of her.'

Kitty started wailing again with more protests at being treated unfairly until Mrs Gardiner intervened and ushered them both from the room.

'I cannot face Mr Bingley,' said Jane. 'What on earth shall we say?'

'I think we should say nothing for the moment,' said Elizabeth. 'They will find out sooner or later, but I cannot give Mr Darcy the satisfaction of seeing the triumph in his face when he realises our family is as degraded as he imagines.'

'Why do you think he would feel that way?' asked Jane. 'Do you suspect him of something? I thought you were getting on so well last night. You made a handsome couple when dancing.'

Lizzy couldn't help chipping in. 'And you admitted that you liked dancing with him very much.'

'I did enjoy dancing with him, but there was one part of our conversation I did not like, that I've puzzled over, but which now seems to make perfect sense.'

'What do you mean?' said Jane. 'Did Mr Darcy give you cause to think he does not like you or our family?'

'He talked at length about how different we are, of his position in society and the inferiority of our situation, but then spoke of his admiration for me, as if all he'd said before might be ignored or disregarded. I told him I did not consider my family to be so very different as to our place and rank, though I admitted he had more money at his disposal.'

'How perfectly horrid and disagreeable of him,' said Jane.

'What is more, I suspect him of keeping you and Mr Bingley apart. He was also very vocal on the behaviour of my sisters, and even our mother. But, I must admit, though I felt inordinately wounded, I knew there to be some truth in his words, and I could not protest as much as I would have liked.'

Elizabeth paused, but she could speak no more as Mr Darcy and Mr Bingley were announced. They came in, but refused a chair. Lizzy noted Mr Darcy's eyes never left Eliza's face, whilst the latter seemed hardly to acknowledge him, keeping her eyes on her lap.

'Forgive us for calling so early,' Mr Darcy began, 'but we could not delay. It is a delicate subject, but I suspect from the expressions of dismay you wear upon your countenances that you have already received the bad news we thought should be communicated to you as soon as possible.'

Jane and Lizzy exchanged glances, but neither spoke.

'Your sister has eloped with Mr Wickham, we understand,' said Mr Bingley, addressing Jane, particularly, in a soft voice.

Elizabeth burst into tears as Jane alluded to it, and for a few minutes neither could speak another word. Darcy, in wretched suspense, could only say something indistinctly of his concern, and observed them both in silence. 'We were grieved, indeed, to hear this dreadful news,' cried Darcy at last, 'Tell me, what has been attempted to recover her?'

Elizabeth spoke. 'My father and uncle are gone to Brighton, but nothing can be done - I know very well that nothing can be done. How are they even to be discovered? I have not the smallest hope!'

Darcy made no answer. He seemed scarcely to hear her, and was walking up and down the room in earnest meditation, his air gloomier than ever. Elizabeth, Jane and Lizzy looked to the other, each coming to the same conclusion. Everything must sink under such a proof of family weakness, an assurance of the deepest disgrace. Lizzy noted the look of further distress on Elizabeth's countenance and could guess what she was thinking. Eliza must realise she has been in love with him all along, Lizzy thought, but suspects love must now be in vain.

Elizabeth and Jane were soon lost to everything else; and, after a pause of several minutes, were only recalled to the situation by Mr Darcy's voice. 'I am afraid you have been long desiring our absence, nor have we anything to plead in excuse of our stay, but real, though unavailing, concern. Would to Heaven that anything could be either said or done on our part that might offer consolation to such distress! But we will not torment you with vain wishes, which may seem purposely to ask for your thanks. This unfortunate affair will, I fear, prevent our sisters from having the pleasure of seeing you later today.'

'Oh yes, be so kind as to apologise to Miss Darcy and Miss Bingley on our behalf. Say that urgent business calls us home immediately. Conceal the unhappy truth as long as it is possible. I know it cannot be long.'

Mr Darcy readily assured them of their secrecy, again expressed his sorrow for their distress, wished it a happier conclusion than there was at present reason to hope, and leaving his compliments for her relations, with only one serious, parting look, went away.

'And that is that, I suppose,' said Elizabeth. 'We shall never see them again.'

'No,' said Jane wearily, 'and our prospects for attracting any young men must now be negligible after our sister's behaviour.'

'I never perceived that Lydia had any partiality for Mr Wickham, and he certainly seemed to have none for her,' Lizzy went on. 'He thoroughly misled us all with his fine ways and easy manners, and I should never have thought him capable of such a crime. Lydia wanted only encouragement to attach herself to anybody; we all know that. Sometimes one officer, sometimes another, were her favourite, her affections were continually fluctuating, but I never suspected she was so attached to Wickham, and he looked set to marry Mary King.'

'And now we must all suffer. I am glad to be going home, though if you'd asked me yesterday I should have said the very opposite,' said Jane reaching for her handkerchief again and bursting into tears.

Lizzy looked on in despair, but knew not how she could make it better, and seeing the sisters turn to one another in distress felt she should leave them alone in their grief.

She made her way upstairs to sort out her things and pack. Everything felt so awful and sad after such happiness and hope. Collecting her belongings together, Lizzy packed the trunk as best as she could. The calendar was the last item to go in and as she placed it on top she thought now might be as good a time as any to open the door of number twenty. It was a painting of a house, but not any old house. It was her home, the terraced house in High Barnet on the outskirts of London where she pictured her mum and dad, and her sister Lily. She wasn't usually a sentimental girl, but right now all she wanted was to be curled up on the sofa next to her mum, and reading her favourite book where it all worked out with happy endings for them all. She could not see that possibility for either Jane, Elizabeth or even herself, and for the first time, she wept real tears, which simply wouldn't cease, no matter how many times she told herself to stop being so silly.

Chapter 21

Door Number *Twenty One*

Piling into the carriage at last, Lizzy was rather dreading the journey home. On the way to Derbyshire it had taken such a long time, and the thought of staying in strange inns and hotels was a very sobering one. Everyone was out of humour, and even Elizabeth who was always so good-natured seemed completely out of sorts. It didn't help that they were so squashed in together, with no room at all for stretching one's legs.

'To think we are going home in such circumstances as this, when I thought at least two of my daughters would be respectably married by now,' wailed Mrs Bennet. 'Well, it's not your sister Lydia who is to blame, as I see it. If you'd consented to Mr Collins' offer in the first place, Lizzy, and you'd made your feelings plainer a lot sooner, Jane, we would have had no need of going anywhere and poor Lydia might have been saved.'

'Mama, that is most unfair,' Elizabeth spoke up immediately. 'You cannot blame us for Lydia's behaviour. She has become more unruly with every passing day, and you've done nothing to correct her wild ways.'

'Lydia was never going to be completely happy until she'd exposed herself in some public place,' added Mary, 'and I fear no correction would have altered the case. The road to ruin was clearly marked, in my opinion, and set in stone a long time ago.'

Elizabeth sighed with exasperation, and Lizzy saw Jane take her sister's hand to give it a squeeze in sympathy.

'It is Jane I feel most sorry for because I know Mr Bingley wanted to make amends,' said Eliza.

'Well, I am sure he will not be calling again, and I daresay his sister will be feeling perfectly justified that she saw fit to warn him off in the first place,' said Jane. 'Mr Bingley and Mr Darcy will want nothing to do with us or our family, I am sure.'

'Not that I care for Mr Darcy's opinions, good or otherwise,' Eliza rejoined. 'I had thought him to be improving on me, but he thinks he is a cut above us. It is disappointing to learn that a young man who has everything in his favour, good looks, money, and position in society, is merely a proud coxcomb.'

'You have never said you found him handsome before,' said Jane with a teasing look. 'Perhaps those angry protestations are masking your true feelings.'

'Mr Darcy has made no impression on my heart, I can assure you, though I hate to think of him despising me, and my family. I cannot bear to think of him congratulating himself on his superior status, and thinking he was right to condemn me. Anyway, I had some satisfaction in telling him he was rather ill-mannered to speak to me in such a disparaging way.'

'Did you really?' Lizzy asked, speaking up for the first time since they'd set off.

'I told him his design was in offending and insulting me, and his manners had impressed me with the fullest belief of his arrogance, his conceit, and his selfish disdain for the feelings of others.'

'You did not spare his feelings then,' said Jane with a smile.

'I did not, especially when he confided that he'd been the reason Mr Bingley had gone to London. Apparently, a "friend" who knew Caroline

Bingley told Mr Darcy about you and Bingley at Chawton. Mr Darcy was as keen to distract him as Miss Bingley, and make a better match for his friend.'

'Mr Darcy tried to persuade Mr Bingley to forget all about me? Is that what you're saying?'

'Apparently, so I think it's plain how much Mr Bingley really does admire you. Even his great friend could not influence him in the end.'

No one spoke again, and they all became very quiet. Jane kept her gaze averted by looking out through the window, and Elizabeth took up a book like Mary. Kitty lolled against her mother, and it wasn't long before they'd both fallen asleep, Mrs Bennet whimpering as she dreamed, lifting the lace on her pelisse with the occasional snore, which made her jump wide awake until sleep stole over her once more.

Lizzy was pensive. Such a lot had happened in the last three weeks, and she'd grown so used to her new life she could hardly recall her old one. It was almost like looking back at someone else's past, and she knew time was running out for her in this existence. There were but three days before Christmas day, and she would really have to try and get home. No matter what her mother had said about stopping as long as she liked, it wouldn't seem right, and she dreaded outstaying her welcome. Part of her couldn't bear to see Jane and Elizabeth so unhappy, and she couldn't work out how the situation could possibly be improved. Darcy and Eliza were at loggerheads, and Bingley was clearly under his friend's influence. Lizzy couldn't imagine, after what Darcy had said to Elizabeth at the ball, that he'd be playing any part in helping the situation, and she wondered if Miss Austen had decided, in the end, to write her real, unexpurgated version.

Thinking about Miss Austen made Lizzy question if she'd stayed behind with the Gardiners at Darley Manor, but a glance through the rear window of the coach satisfied her curiosity. Just as before, the bright yellow paint of the post chaise informed her that Jane was not far behind, and Lizzy wondered if she felt pleased to be going back to Chawton. Perhaps when Jane had had a chance to revise her writing she might find a way through the muddle. Lizzy settled back against the cushioned seat, gradually succumbing to the rhythm of the horses' hooves drumming along the roads and highways.

Closing her eyes she gave in to sleep which sucked her down a long, dark tunnel of nightmares. Her dreams were fretful and too frighteningly real: in one of them she was kidnapped by robbers, who stopped the coach at gunpoint, and there he was again, intruding on her dreams. Mr Williams was masked, and wielding a silver pistol, holding it against her throat. She could smell his cologne; feel his breath on her face, and the touch of his long tapered fingers, cold to the touch, as he took her gold hoops from her ears. His eyes held hers, and the look was so intense she could not maintain it. He laughed … a cruel, mocking laugh, that was so loud the sound made her start and jump out of her skin, bringing her back to consciousness, before she opened her eyes with relief. Her heart was hammering, and she felt frightened with a sense of unease prickling over her skin, as if all of a sudden she didn't know where she belonged and what the future held for her.

Lizzy had to pinch herself at first because although she knew exactly where she was, it was so unexpected. As she looked around taking in her surroundings, unable to believe quite what she was seeing and hearing, her ears tuned in to the modern world, which intruded in all its jangling, colourful noisiness. Lying in her bed at home, with the sounds of the television blaring downstairs, and the noisy engines of cars roaring up and down the High Street, a few hundred feet away, felt familiar but totally wrong. And whilst it was rather comforting to see all her possessions, the books and the detritus on her dressing table, clothes abandoned on a chair, the photos of her beloved Granny and her favourite scent, which she'd longed to have in that other time, she felt utterly confused. How could she possibly be back, she wondered? Life with the Bennets had been so real, and now it seemed the episode had been nothing but a dream. The thought that she wouldn't be spending more time with Elizabeth and Jane really made her feel very sad, and she really began to doubt that any of it had happened. How ridiculous to imagine there was some sort of alternative universe where you could live alongside characters from your favourite books. She'd totally lost it, this time, she thought.

But then she saw the calendar propped up against her bedside light, obscuring the gilt alarm clock with the fancy scrolls and arabesques that her father had brought back from Austria when she was a small child. The calendar was no figment of her deranged mind, it was real and tangible, and as she examined it closely, all the pictures were there intact. Number twenty-one was softly lit, and when she opened the door, she could have cried. The little animated scene showed Jane and Elizabeth standing outside Chawton cottage. They were waving madly, as if their lives depended on it, and blowing kisses to her, so she knew in that moment that dream or not, it had all been as real as any experience could be.

Chapter 22

Door Number *Twenty Two*

It was quite early the next day when her mum came in with a breakfast tray, on which were arranged a glass of orange, a poached egg on toast, and a pot of Earl Grey tea. Lizzy propped herself against the pillows while her mother fussed round.

'How are you, Lizzy? I didn't like to disturb you last night you were so shattered, but I understand from Mrs Bennet's note you had a bit of a journey for the first half to Chawton with awful hold ups all along the motorway. What a kind lady to send you home from there in a taxi, we'll have to send the fare back - it must have cost such a lot!'

Lizzy watched her mum arranging the tray, and tucking her up as if she were a little girl. It was rather lovely to be so cosseted, and she suddenly realised how much she'd missed her. Even though she had a habit of interfering in everything she did, and telling Lizzy what was best, she knew she had a large heart, and that she was loved. If her mum had spoilt Lily, it was because she thought she was showing her how much she loved her, and though Lizzy knew her sister really needed a firm hand, she knew her mother's actions had always been wrought out of affection for them both.

'I don't remember most of the journey home,' Lizzy said truthfully, unable to make head or tail of the motorway and taxi story. 'I think I just slept.'

'Too many late nights, by the sounds of things, but I'm glad you took my advice and enjoyed yourself. You did have a lovely time, didn't you? You haven't come back early because …'

'No, Mum, nothing happened that you have anything to be concerned about. They all had to go back to Chawton, and it just felt like the end of the holiday, I suppose.'

Lizzy couldn't explain it any better than that. She didn't feel like going into great lengths of detail about what had happened to Lydia, or Jane and Elizabeth. It had been a magical experience, for the most part, but now it was over, and she just wanted to get back to normal. Lizzy remembered last night's picture in the calendar - she was glad to see they'd all been smiling. They looked happy, and that was the picture she wanted to keep in her head, even if she might not know how everything was going to turn out. Even though she was sure they were being brave, she knew if the sisters didn't succeed with the men they loved, they would always have one another. Lizzy felt so sad at the thought she might not see them again or know what happened in the end. At least she still had the calendar to remind her of the extraordinary days she'd spent with those friends who now seemed so far away, and in a time that was so elusive.

'Stay in bed as long as you like - Dad thought you might like to get the Christmas tree later - go and see Mrs Dale at the farm.'

Lizzy smiled. 'I wouldn't miss that for the world. I won't be long, Mum, and tell Dad I'd love to go with him.'

'I knew you would. Well, enjoy your egg, and I'll catch up with you a bit later. You can tell me all about your trip then.'

Lizzy knew she wasn't going to get away with saying nothing at all about it. 'Yes, I think you'll enjoy hearing about the amazing houses I've seen.'

'Yes, I'd love that. I think Lily said her friend's family in Brighton live in a pretty big house too, but you know what she's like, she doesn't give a lot away.'

'Have you heard anything since she went, Mum?'

Mrs Benson sat down on the bed. Lizzy had never seen her look so worried. 'She's doing her usual, not answering her phone. I'm sure if she knew how worried I was she'd answer it. I don't know what to do, Lizzy, I don't know the address where she's staying, or Harriet's surname and phone number. I didn't think to find out before she left, and you know what's she's like wanting her independence and not being babied.'

'I know, Mum, but she is only just sixteen.'

'She went off before I knew it, and then just texted me to say she wasn't coming back.'

'Leave it with me. I know some of her friends, and I'll see if I can find out anything. It's likely her phone is dead and she didn't take her charger with her. She wouldn't think about you worrying.'

'Thank you, Lizzy,' said her mum, patting her hand. 'It's lovely to have you home - I have missed you. And I'm sure Lily will be fine - she'll turn up sooner or later.'

Lizzy turned to the calendar when her mum had gone. She hoped opening the door might give her some more news or pictures of her friends, but there was nothing but the painting of a beautiful Christmas tree looking very much like the one they always put up in the corner of the sitting room. Even so, she felt a tingle of excitement. It was Christmas, after all, and she loved nothing so well as a Christmas tree.

Lizzy got up and dressed shortly after her breakfast, and took herself off to the High Street where she knew Lily's friends hung out in one of the coffee shops, pretending they were much older and trying out the make up they'd bought. But, it seemed they had other things to occupy them today and she couldn't find a single one of them. But, it was so close to Christmas, and very cold. More than likely they'd de-camped to one of their houses, and she wasn't sure where any of them lived. Lizzy abandoned that idea deciding not to think about it until later. She knew that letting problems simmer often helped to produce wonderful solutions, and that before the end of the day she was sure she would have resolved the predicament of what to do for the best about Lily. In the meantime, she had her dad to worry about. She'd only seen him briefly, but he looked so worried and despondent. A man of few words, she knew he was finding it hard to decide what to do for the best.

Going to the farm in the afternoon with her dad was lovely. It was a ritual Lizzy had never grown out of, and the smell of the pine needles was enough to restore some feelings of happiness as they lingered over Mr Dale's selection of trees.

'This one has a lovely shape,' said Mr Benson.

'Yes,' agreed Lizzy, 'but it's not tall enough, and you know how Lily always loves the tree to be scraping the ceiling.'

Her father laughed, before he turned to face her looking rather sad. 'Yes, I thought she might have come back this morning. She always loves choosing the tree and trimming it. I've never known her to miss it before, but she did say she wouldn't be back until after Christmas. I'm afraid of pushing her away, Lizzy, if you know what I mean. The more I try and keep her close, the more she keeps her distance.'

'It's her age, Dad, I'm sure she'll grow out of it,' Lizzy said turning to give him a big hug. 'Next year she'll be with us again, you'll see.'

Lily wasn't mentioned after that, and they chose the best tree with her in mind, tying it onto the car roof and securing it with rope. Lizzy and her father were both quiet on the journey home. How could she be so selfish, Lizzy thought, and not for the first time did she feel cross with her little sister.

Decorating the tree and trimming the mantelpiece were always lovely tasks, and fetching out the precious ornaments were a joy. Many were made of glass and porcelain, ancient baubles that had miraculously survived the odd occasion when a new kitten had gone scrambling up the branches or the time when the tree had simply fallen over in the night with a huge crash making them all wake in alarm thinking the house was being burgled. Unwrapping every precious decoration from its nest of tissue paper brought forth surprises of forgotten delights. There were glittering angels, glass birds with exotic feathers, Father Christmases dressed in red, and Jane Austen baubles filled with quotes from her favourite book. When she took out a sparkling skating figure dressed in a red fur-lined cloak, she couldn't help thinking about the day when Mr Williams had been his most charming. She remembered his smile, and the way his eyes crinkled at the corners when she was clearly amusing him in some way. What was he doing right now, she wondered? That was the trouble with Christmas she thought. It was easy to spend too much time on memories and looking back.

Chapter 23

Door Number *Twenty Three*

Lizzy was beginning to lose interest in the calendar with everything that was going on, but it was a habit she couldn't entirely put aside, and with there being only two days left to open, she automatically turned to it the moment she woke up. Today's offering was a lovely picture of a toy snowstorm like the ones she'd taken out of their Christmas boxes the day before and arranged on the mantelshelf with garlands of pine and sprigs of holly. Another child-like treat, she had collected different examples of the glass globes, each containing a fairytale world, every year since she was a little girl. The one in the painting zoomed into focus, and she saw the pavilion trapped inside, the incongruous yet beautiful palace built by the Prince Regent in Brighton.

As if she were being pulled into the picture, and the globe itself, for a moment she felt the snow swirling round her shoulders and saw it settle on the onion domes, she smelled the tang of the sea and heard the mournful cry of gulls who soared on the wind.

Finding her cheeks wet with tears, Lizzy could not stop thinking about

Lily. Call it a second sense, or something like it, the sisters had always shared a special bond growing up, and it was like a signal going off in her head whenever Lily was in trouble. She felt it now, even more so as the snow still twirled about the snowstorm palace, but she had no idea what to do about it. Unable to turn to her best friend, she felt the need to talk it over and thrash out the problem, more than ever, but came very sadly to the conclusion she had no one close enough she could share it with.

When Lizzy went downstairs she found her mum making sausage rolls in the kitchen. It was one of Lizzy's favourite traditions that they ate them following the afternoon carol service on Christmas Eve, and the smells from the oven made her feel hungry.

'There's always so much to do, isn't there?' her mother exclaimed. 'The cake is ready for icing if you'd like to help out.'

Lizzy busied herself making the royal icing, and managed to get most of it on top of the cake without sticking her finger in, for a taste, too often. 'Perhaps we'll have a smooth top this year, Mum,' she said, fetching out the palette knife and dipping it into a jug of hot water.

'Anything you like!' her mum called, stopping to rub the flour off her hands on a tea towel as the phone rang.

Sticking out her tongue in concentration, Lizzy smoothed the icing on top of the cake and down the sides, but she'd hardly started when her mother appeared again, phone in hand, but covering the mouthpiece so the person on the other end couldn't hear.

'It's Mr Williams!' said Mrs Benson.

Lizzy saw her mother had turned pink, but she often did that when she spoke to young men she liked.

'I don't want to talk to him,' answered Lizzy, feeling totally bewildered. Wasn't he just someone she'd conjured up out of her imagination or wasn't he simply the product of someone else's? If she was honest, all Mr Williams had ever been was a kind of watered down Mr Darcy without any redeeming features, whatsoever, apart from the ability to kiss her into oblivion. 'Tell him I'm not here.'

'I can't do that, I've already told him you are here!'

'Well, tell him I've just popped out.'

For a moment Lizzy thought she'd got away with it, as she saw her mum start to speak.

'Just a moment, Mr Williams. Yes, it's fine, not at all inconvenient … yes, she's right here.' With that, Mrs Benson held out the phone to her daughter and glared. Lizzy knew that expression of old, and knew she had no choice. Reluctantly, she took the phone, but didn't speak until she was safely in her room.

'Hello,' she said hesitantly.

'Hi, Lizzy,' said the voice she hardly recognised. He sounded so informal and well … so friendly.

She couldn't speak, and when he spoke again, for some inexplicable reason she felt a lump in her throat, and tears in her eyes.

'I hope you're okay. I'm really sorry I haven't been in touch, but there was a bit of work I had to sort out.'

'Oh that's fine, it wasn't your fault you had to go home.' The conversation was so surreal she could hardly believe she was actually hearing his voice.

'Look, I know I was really grumpy on that last day in Derbyshire - I didn't mean to be, I was just really cross about having to go back, and the truth is … I knew I was going to miss you.'

Time stopped, and everything ceased in that moment. There were no sounds except for the thumping of her heart and the ticking of the clock eerily beating time in harmony. Had she possibly heard correctly? Had he said something about missing her?

'Lizzy, are you there?'

'Yes, I'm still here.'

'I hope you don't mind me saying that.'

'Don't mind you saying what?'

'The bit about missing you. Forgive me for saying this over the phone, but the truth is I'd never have the courage to say it to your face. I'm not very good at telling people how I feel, not very good at emotions in general, to tell the truth, but I want you to know I've really missed you, and I was hoping you might have missed me just a little bit.'

It was so lovely to hear his voice, but when she spoke she was so quiet as hardly to be heard. 'I have missed you.'

'Have you really?'

'Yes.' Lizzy could hardly speak. She couldn't remember ever having such a surreal conversation in her life before. And then he started telling her about his work and what he'd been doing, and suddenly she was opening up to him too. Before she knew what she'd done she'd told him all about Lily and how worried she was about her.

'She's in Brighton?' he asked.

'Yes, I know she was staying with a friend's family, but I don't know if that's the case any longer. I've got no proof of anything, just a really uneasy feeling that something isn't right.'

'And you don't know exactly where she's staying.'

'No, that sounds dreadful, doesn't it? The only thing I remember her mentioning was Sir Laurence Olivier.'

'The actor?'

'Yes, he starred in the old black and white film of *Pride and Prejudice* - always a favourite of my darling Granny. I admit, I wasn't really listening to her properly, and I can't think why she mentioned him because he's no longer with us, unless her friend's father knew him years ago. I really don't know. Anyway, I don't think it's much of a clue.'

'No, doesn't sound like it ... well ... I'm sorry I can't help you, but I've loved talking to you, Lizzy.'

He suddenly sounded rather distant and abrupt, as if he couldn't wait to get off the phone.

'I'll be in touch ... take care,' he said.

She didn't have time to answer. Lizzy heard the click, and they were cut off. Perhaps she'd said too much about her wayward sister, Lizzy thought. She didn't know what to think except it seemed obvious he'd been fine until she'd told him about Lily, and then he couldn't wait to get off the phone. She just couldn't think straight any more. After a few more minutes Lily went back down to the kitchen.

'Everything all right?' her mother asked. Lizzy saw with some amusement that the cake she'd started icing no longer had a smooth top. Her mother was fashioning the usual crispy tufts and waves that Lizzy really had a fondness for, and she walked to the kitchen counter to lend a hand with the plethora of decorations for the top. None of them were to scale, she thought, but she rather liked the sight of the giant robin next to the miniature cottage, which grew ever smaller with each passing year as the icing was nibbled off the bottom just a little bit more, along with a layer of plaster. The snowman and the super-sized holly leaves finished it all off to perfection, which no smoothly iced confection with a plain white ribbon could ever match, Lizzy thought.

'Yes, everything's fine. He just phoned to see if I got home all right,' she said, knowing she was not telling the whole truth.

'He's a nice young man,' said Mrs Benson, and looked at her daughter with a grin before bending her head to the task of tying a scarlet ribbon round her creation. 'You could do a lot worse …'

Chapter 24

Door Number *Twenty Four*

When Lizzy woke the next morning, she was resolved on a new plan. Lying there worrying about her sister was not going to achieve anything, and why she hadn't thought about travelling down to Brighton before she couldn't think. She could easily get a train, and get there in no time at all. It was the only option open to her, and she was sure she'd find Lily as easily as bumping into her on the pier. There wouldn't even be any reason to tell her parents, she'd just say she was visiting friends, and would be back later. And what better present for her mum and dad than to bring her sister home for Christmas! She felt better now she had a plan of action, and she leapt out of bed with a renewed purpose.

'You'll come with us to see Jenny and Caroline, won't you?' her mother asked.

Lizzy knew that to dismiss these particular traditions would break her mother's heart. Mince pies, a glass or two of sherry, and present swapping with her mother's closest friends was a Christmas Eve ritual as firmly entrenched as those of Christmas Day itself. She would just have to catch the later train, but she couldn't see how she would be able to escape until the afternoon, at least. When her mum asked if she'd help with some last minute present wrapping, she threw herself into the task, knowing that the quicker they were wrapped up, the quicker they'd be given away.

Wrapping up the most awkwardly shaped parcels she'd ever seen was taking much longer than she hoped, and another strike of the clock on the mantelpiece told her another hour had passed. It was almost two o'clock in the afternoon, and she knew as soon as the presents were delivered that her mother would be talking about the carol concert, and she wouldn't be able to get out of that either. It was just possible she could slip off afterwards and catch an evening train. Of course, it might mean she'd have to phone her parents later and tell them what she'd done, but if it meant she could go off without worrying them too much, that seemed the best way forward.

It was three o'clock by the time she was just tearing off the last strip of sticky tape with her teeth, to line up with the others on the edge of the glass table in the sitting room, and battling with a length of Christmas wrap that would keep rolling back up, when the doorbell rang. Running to the hall so she could get back to her wrapping quickly, she opened the front door, and received the shock of her life.

There was Lily on the doorstep, looking contrite for once in her life, but more astonishing than to see her sister was the person behind her, standing at some distance. Lizzy actually felt her mouth drop open. She just stood there not knowing what to do or say until her mother's arrival made enough noise and fuss for the pair of them.

Lily was whisked away by Mrs Benson into the warmth of the sitting room. Lizzy doubted she'd even noticed that Mr Williams was standing behind Lily, still out in the freezing cold, not that her mother even knew what he looked like. And when she looked at him now, Lizzy felt she hardly recognised him herself. He was still as tall with those handsome dark looks, but he looked younger, somehow, in blue jeans and a crisp, white shirt. He wore a grey jumper to match his eyes, thrown casually over his shoulders and the sight of him actually made her heart leap.

'Hi Lizzy.'

'Hi.' For the first time, Lizzy didn't know what to call him. It seemed too silly to call him Mr Williams and far too formal.

'May I come in?' he asked. 'I ought to explain to your mother, and I'd like to introduce myself, if that's okay.'

Lizzy could hardly speak. He looked so gorgeous, and he spoke so softly, and his mouth smiled at her the whole time, as his eyes kept drinking her in until she felt she'd be consumed by one more glance. She loved the feeling and when he stepped inside the hallway, he leaned into her and kissed her on the cheek. How she didn't collapse in a heap like the melting snowman in the street outside, she didn't know, but she kissed him back, and felt the pleasure of his hand in the small of her back pulling her closer.

'How on earth did you find her?' Lizzy managed to say at last, as he pulled away.

'It was when you mentioned Sir Laurence Olivier. I remembered reading that he'd had a house on the Royal Crescent in Brighton, and I wondered if Lily's friend might live close by. It didn't take me long to get down there, and make some enquiries. Lily hadn't gone far, though she and her friend had concocted a story about staying together, which wasn't true. She was, in fact, with a young boy about her age - she said you know him.'

'George?'

'Yes, he's the one. Well, I expect she'll tell you about it, but she's promised me she won't go running off again, and I've said she must learn to concentrate on her studies instead.'

'Good luck with that, I'm afraid you don't know my sister very well.'

'Perhaps, though a little bribery goes a long way, I've found. I've promised her a weekly outing in my car at her request.'

Lizzy looked beyond the open door at the sports car parked on the road. She hadn't a clue about smart cars, but she could see instantly that her sister would have been very impressed.

'And I expect one of her conditions is that you drop her round to her friends' houses or meet-ups?'

'How could you possibly know that?' he asked with a twinkle in his eye.

'Oh dear,' Lizzy couldn't help but laugh. 'I hope you won't regret it.'

'Not if it means I can see you more often. Would you let me take you out sometimes?'

Lizzy nodded. 'I'd love that, but I have my conditions too.'

'Name them - anything - ask away, Lizzy.'

'I can't keep calling you Mr Williams,' said Lizzy. 'I know your name begins with the letter D because my mother told me. Is it David?'

Mr Williams shook his head and grinned. 'No, it's Darcy.'

Lizzy laughed. 'You're joking, right? Darcy Williams?'

'I wish I were. What can I say in my defence? *Pride and Prejudice* is my mother's favourite novel. But, you can call me Dara, most people do - it's a kind of shortened version I came up with when I was old enough to be teased for being named Darcy. I am half Irish so I guess it fits. Can I meet your mum and dad now? I feel I know your mother already, we've been getting on so well with our correspondence.'

Of course, when Lizzy's mum met Dara, it was plain even if Lizzy hadn't fallen for him on her first impressions, her mother certainly had. It was very surreal watching them both, and Lizzy couldn't help admiring the way he seemed to have both her sister and her mum eating out of his hand. It wasn't long before they were all talking and laughing like old friends, and she could see how impressed her dad was by him, shaking his hand vigorously, clapping him on the back, and getting out his best malt whisky.

When it was time to go visiting and delivering parcels, Lizzy's mum took her to one side, and suggested she could manage on her own. Surprisingly, she said, it seemed Lily was keen to go in Lizzy's place, and even her father had volunteered to help carry the presents.

'I can't thank him enough,' said Mrs Benson, 'what your Dara has done for us.'

'He's not my Dara, Mum.'

'Well, I think he is ... anyway, it's a miracle. I feel as if I've got my baby back.'

Lizzy smiled. She really hoped that was the case, and it did seem as if Lily was keen to help. Not much had been mentioned about her friend George, though Lizzy was sure she'd hear all about it at some point.

'And Lizzy, he is so very handsome ... and very ...'

'Mum!'

'Just saying ...'

The house seemed very quiet with her parents and Lily gone, and when she walked into the sitting room with that ridiculous over-dressed tree dominating the room, she wondered what Dara could possibly make of the whole episode, and of her family. He was sitting on the sofa, and she hesitated a moment, before deciding to sit next to him.

'My mother is beyond words of gratitude,' she said, just managing to gaze into the eyes that were fixed steadily on hers. 'We all are ... it's as if you've performed a sort of Christmas magic trick, bringing Lily back, especially as she seems so polite and co-operative under your influence.'

'Oh, Lizzy, it was nothing, and you must know I did it all for you. I treated you badly before, I was unforgivably rude when all along I knew in my heart that I was falling in love with you. I had to find a way to make it up to you, and this seemed the perfect opportunity.'

Lizzy saw the sincerity in his eyes, and when he held out his hand she didn't resist, placing her fingers on his outstretched palm. He closed his fingers over hers and pulled her, so she had no choice but to nestle down next to him, and rested her head just under his chin.

'There are so many things I need to ask you,' Lizzy began. 'I am really struggling with the idea of everything that's happened, and how it was possible.'

She couldn't think how to go on, he'd think her completely mad, she was sure, if she tried to put into words everything she felt she'd experienced.

'It will all come out in time. You just need to trust your feelings, and your instincts, Lizzy. Magical things do happen, you know.'

'But, you're real. You're not a character in a book, and yet, I feel you were there and living it all as much as me.'

'We lived every second, Lizzy, and I hope there'll be many more such moments. There is a particular kind of enchantment that is unique to your favourite author, and the house where she lived, that's the only way I can explain it. I think everyone who visits or works there feels that, as does anyone who reads her books to some extent or other. There are just different levels to it, I suppose, and only a very privileged few ever go beyond what they see with their eyes. You have a talent for seeing far and above the ordinary, Lizzy, as well as into the hearts and minds of those you love, and can pick up on the sort of vibrations most ordinary people miss altogether.'

'And you are the same!' said Lizzy, sitting up to look back at him, understanding just what he meant. 'Though, I must admit, on first impression, I would not have thought you were a sensitive type.'

'Maybe not,' Dara said with a wry smile, 'but I'm very choosy about who I let into my life and the worlds I inhabit. I was just making sure you were the right person.'

Lizzy reached for the nearest cushion and took aim. 'Oh, and arrogance is your middle name, I think! I really do wonder if you've known Jane Austen a lot longer than you let on, for it's clear she must have based a certain character on your very own.'

Dara laughed. 'It's true, we go back a long way. But, looking into the past is not why I'm here today. It's the future I'm thinking about. God, Lizzy, I missed you so much.'

Lizzy felt her insides melting, and when he pulled her closer, she did nothing to resist.

When Lizzy looked back over the day, it was hard to believe what had happened. Dara had brought Lily home; he'd found and rescued her, going all the way to Brighton like a detective would, or like Mr Darcy in *Pride and Prejudice*. And not only that, but he'd turned out to be quite as lovely as he'd been in her dreams, except the one about the highway man, of course. Lizzy could hardly sleep she was so excited. It wasn't only the thought of Christmas Day to come that filled her thoughts with such pleasure, but knowing he slept in the guest bedroom just down the landing was also keeping her very much awake. At her parents' insistence he'd been invited to stay, and it seemed to Lizzy he was very happy to accept. Before they'd parted, he'd said goodnight, and handed her a Christmas parcel, which he said could only be opened, in private, the next morning. Lizzy had tried very hard not to squeeze it, and put it next to the calendar on the bedside table to open first thing. She wished she had something to give him, but had a feeling there might be other opportunities to come.

When she opened the last door of the calendar it came as no surprise to see the picture of two little girls, their heads closely together, smiling with pride at the nativity scene they'd just assembled. Lit by candlelight, the little figures glowed like magic. Mary, in blue, held her precious baby in her arms, as Joseph, the wise men, shepherds, and the angels looked on. The younger of the two girls had a cheeky face, and looked up to her big sister with admiring eyes. The elder had her arm protectively draped round the shoulders of the little one, and was doing her best not to smile too widely for fear of exposing the gap where her two front teeth had been.

Lizzy felt suddenly elated! It was so good to feel that everything was coming together at last - Lily was safe and content once more, her mum and dad were happy beyond words, and the man of her dreams was just a step or two away.

Chapter 25

Christmas Day

There was nothing so exciting as waking on Christmas Day in the early hours, and feeling for a knobbly stocking at the end of her bed, Lizzy thought. Her mother often threatened to withdraw this family favourite, and had even succeeded once, but the sisters had protested so much it had been immediately reinstated the following year. The stocking might be a childish whim, but finding a sugar mouse in the toe, a bag of chocolate coins and a Father Christmas wrapped in bright foil were the highlights of the morning, even if she was twenty-one and old enough to know better. She couldn't help wondering if Dara was awake, and if her mother had managed to cobble a stocking together for him. Lizzy would have put money on the fact that she had - her mother was always prepared for any eventuality.

The parcel next to her bed looked just as mysterious as it had the night before. When she started unwrapping it there were so many layers she didn't think she'd ever get to the bottom of them. The last were of soft tissue paper and when she peeled them away, she could see it was a file of papers wrapped in a cloth covering, that looked like a piece of embroidered muslin taken from an old gown. Pulling them out carefully, she saw there was a title page, and a letter placed on top. The handwriting looked most familiar.

> Dear Lizzy,
> How can I thank you enough for your invaluable help? I could not have resolved it all without you or indeed seen what was always under my nose. You would think, having the same one as my mother and rather long, that seeing under my nose would be an easy task, but it often seems to me that we overlook what is plainly there all along.
> I have enclosed my manuscript – it is a wretched piece in comparison to the novel I am lopping and cropping now, but I thought you might enjoy having a copy, as a keepsake, and that you would like to see some of the revisions I made towards the end of the book. I find endings and beginnings great fun to write, but I fear there is still much to be improved in the middle.
> Your friend, Mr Williams, was of great assistance to me. I must admit, I've not always been so successful in finding a suitable role for him, but if I might refer again to noses, he is yet another example of being there, but not always noticed by yours truly. I am sorry to have taken him away from you just as you were beginning to know one another, but I needed him to help transcribe and edit some of these passages and pages. He truly has been the great hero of the hour, and one that will never be bettered, I am sure. It was his idea to leave the Advent calendar in the shop though I didn't really believe it would work as well as it did. But, thank goodness, it brought you to our door. He always said there'd be another Elizabeth, and of course, he was quite right.
> I hope you will come and visit us again at Chawton cottage one of the days. I wish you all the compliments of the season and I remain,
> Yours ever,
> Miss J. Austen.

A letter from Miss Austen! Lizzy could hardly believe her eyes or the sentiments it contained, and knew she would treasure it always. She couldn't wait any longer to read the manuscript, taking note of the top sheet, which looked a little like a title page, but with many crossings out. The top title said *First Impressions*, in large capitals, but that had been crossed out very thoroughly, and then there was a long list of others, which must also have been under consideration at one time, all struck through with lines of brown ink: *Mr Darcy's Secret, Mr Darcy's Pledge, A Fair Prospect, Mr Darcy came to Dinner, Darcy's Decision, Only Mr Darcy Will Do, Mr Darcy's Proposal, Mr Darcy's Little Sister, Becoming Elizabeth Darcy, Mrs Darcy's Dilemma, The Darcys of Derbyshire, The Darcys of Pemberley, Pride, Prejudice and the Perfect Match, Austentatious, The Man Who Loved Jane Austen, The Missing Manuscript of Jane Austen, Definitely Not Mr Darcy*, and last, but by no mans least, *Pride and Prejudice*. Gosh, thought Lizzy, many of the titles threw up more questions than answers, and what a shame they had been passed over, though *Pride and Prejudice*, she was sure, was simply the best!

She skimmed through the chapters, stroking the pages, thrilled to think that Jane Austen's hand had penned the words. It was easy to see the chapters that had been transcribed by Dara - though neat, his handwriting sloped the other way. It was wonderful to see the book she knew in production, and whilst not exactly the same as the one she loved so well, she was thrilled to have been part of its process.

Lydia was married, she was glad to see, and Mr Darcy had been the true hero at the last making sure Wickham stepped up to the mark and married her. That gentleman seemed to have undergone another transformation earlier in the book, Lizzy was pleased to note in the edits, and he was behaving far more like the scoundrel he should be.

When she reached the end, she saw although not finished to the final conclusion, it was one of the many favourite parts of the book she recognised. Here, Lizzy noticed there was little editing and hardly any scribbling out. Lying back against the pile of soft pillows she read every word with pleasure, recognising the words from *Pride and Prejudice*. It was such a wonderful scene, just after Eliza has been walking out with Darcy, and she is ready to confide in Jane.

'My dear Lizzy, where can you have been walking to?' was a question, which Elizabeth received from Jane as soon as she entered the room, and from all the others when they sat down to table. She had only to say in reply, that they had wandered about till she was beyond her

own knowledge. She coloured as she spoke; but neither that, nor anything else, awakened a suspicion of the truth.

The evening passed quietly, unmarked by anything extraordinary. The acknowledged lovers talked and laughed; the unacknowledged were silent. Darcy was not of a disposition in which happiness overflows in mirth; and Elizabeth, agitated and confused, rather knew that she was happy, than felt herself to be so; for, besides the immediate embarrassment, there were other evils before her. She anticipated what would be felt in the family when her situation became known; she was aware that no one liked him but Jane, and even feared that with the others it was a dislike, which not all his fortune and consequence might do away.

At night she opened her heart to Jane. Though suspicion was very far from Miss Bennet's general habits, she was absolutely incredulous here.

'You are joking, Lizzy. This cannot be - engaged to Mr Darcy! - No, no, you shall not deceive me. I know it to be impossible.'

'This is a wretched beginning indeed! My sole dependence was on you; and I am sure nobody else will believe me, if you do not. Yet, indeed, I am in earnest. I speak nothing but the truth. He still loves me, and we are engaged.'

Jane looked at her doubtingly. 'Oh, Lizzy! It cannot be. I know how much you dislike him.'

'You know nothing of the matter. That is all to be forgot. Perhaps I did not always love him so well as I do now. But in such cases as these a good memory is unpardonable. This is the last time I shall ever remember it myself.'

Miss Bennet still looked all amazement. Elizabeth again, and more seriously, assured her of its truth.

'Good Heaven! Can it be really so? Yet now I must believe you,' cried Jane. 'My dear, dear Lizzy, I would - I do congratulate you; but are you certain - forgive the question - are you quite certain that you can be happy with him?'

'There can be no doubt of that. It is settled between us already that we are to be the happiest couple in the world. But are you pleased, Jane? Shall you like to have such a brother?'

'Very, very much. Nothing could give either Bingley or myself more delight. But we considered it, we talked of it as impossible. And do you really love him quite well enough? Oh, Lizzy! Do anything rather than marry without affection. Are you quite sure that you feel what you ought to do?'

'Oh, yes! You will only think I feel more than I ought to do, when I tell you all.'
'What do you mean?'
'Why, I must confess that I love him better than I do Bingley. I am afraid you will be angry.'
'My dearest sister, now be, be serious. I want to talk very seriously. Let me know everything that I am to know without delay. Will you tell me how long you have loved him?'
'It has been coming on so gradually, that I hardly know when it began. But I believe I must date it from my first seeing his beautiful grounds at Pemberley.'
Another intreaty that she would be serious, however, produced the desired effect, and she soon satisfied Jane by her solemn assurances of attachment. When convinced on that article, Miss Bennet had nothing farther to wish.
'Now I am quite happy,' said she, 'for you will be as happy as myself. I always had a value for him. Were it for nothing but his love of you, I must always have esteemed him; but now, as Bingley's friend and your husband, there can be only Bingley and yourself more dear to me ...

There it stopped, but she was quite happy to read what she longed to hear. She was sure that was how it had all turned out at Chawton too! If only she could see Elizabeth and Jane to wish them well. How she would ever thank Dara for bringing this wonderful gift, or equally thank Miss Austen for such a treasure, she had no idea, but she couldn't wait to see him. There was no time to lose.

It was impossible to stay in bed any longer, and though the little gilt clock told her it was only five o'clock in the morning, she pulled on a dressing gown and her smartest slippers, stepping out onto the landing, alert to every sound. On further investigation, she saw the door of his room was open, but he was not inside. Lizzy peered over the banisters. She could see a light glowing down below, beyond the hallway, but she couldn't make out its exact source, so she tiptoed downstairs being careful not to make a noise. The back door was left slightly ajar, and though it was dark along the snowy path running to the back of the garden, she could see a light in the distance. As she passed the first lawn and flower borders she could see a lantern glowing up by the arbour where she could see the figure of a young man sitting in deep thought.

When Dara Williams walked across the grass towards her she could only think just how perfect a Mr Darcy he was to her eyes. Already dressed for the day, she suddenly thought perhaps he'd be shocked to see her standing there in her pyjamas and dressing gown, but he simply smiled, and moving towards her like the Darcy of her dreams he enfolded her into his arms to hold her tightly. His lips on hers, felt sweet and soft as he tenderly kissed her over and again. Nothing had prepared her for this moment, and when she thought of all her other wild imaginings, the kisses that followed simply faded in comparison.

'I love you, Miss Benson,' he said, stroking her hair and pulling her closer. 'Happy Christmas.'

Lizzy looked up to see him studying her face. He stroked her cheek with a finger and traced her mouth before pecking at her lips again and again until she moaned with pleasure.

'Happy Christmas,' she said at last. 'I love you too, Darcy.'

'And you managed to say that without laughing,' he said, kissing the end of her nose.

'Well, personally speaking, I love your name, and I could never laugh at you ... at least, not very often,' Lizzy answered with a smile.

'A good job too, because I could never cope with a humourless wife.'

'What did you say?'

'I was asking you to marry me in a very roundabout way. Will you accept my offer to love you forever?'

'I hardly know you,' Lizzy said, sure that he must be teasing her.

'Perhaps we have not been acquainted for long, as Miss Austen would say, but I think we know one another just as much as we need to, and certainly better than that other couple you're always thinking about.'

'Elizabeth and Darcy?'

'The very same! Now, based on what we know is the most incredible match in the universe, a joyous ending to satisfy all endings, I think we have every chance, Miss Benson, of making a similarly happy marriage, even if you cannot yet make the promise I want to hear. May I hope, after you've spent some time getting to know me, and after thinking about whether you can return my love eternally, that you will consider my proposal? And then after all that, for just however long it takes, do you think you could do me the honour of becoming my wife?'

Lizzy didn't hesitate; she knew the answer in her heart. 'I do, Mr Williams.'

He laughed. 'Ah, grumpy Mr Williams. I think we've seen the last of him. You've taught me so much, Lizzy, and I really am trying to learn not to take life so seriously. I hope you know I'm changed from the proud and arrogant man I used to be.'

'But you are talking as if you are the only person with faults. I was just as guilty of pride and prejudice in my behaviour to you. I promise that you will find I've changed since we've been apart.'

'I would not wish to change a single thing about you,' he said, 'although there is one further request I have to make.'

Lizzy wondered what he could possibly mean, his expression was so serious.

'It's not really about anything to do with changing you; it's to do with you being with me, and at my side. There's to be a double wedding at Chawton, next year, but I would like to make it a triple one before I take you home to Amberley. You must know it's written in the stars, and has been pictured in a magical calendar.'

Lizzy remembered the wedding party drawing up to Amberley House, saw the bride and her groom stepping down from the carriage amidst the cheers of friends, and knew she'd seen her future. She threw her arms round Darcy's neck kissing him over and over. 'If you mean we will be joining Jane and Elizabeth's wedding celebrations I couldn't be more excited.'

'And you will make me the happiest of men if you marry me when summer arrives.'

'Oh, Darcy, I couldn't think of anything more blissful … if only everyone could be as happy as me.'

'You sound like Jane Bennet,' said Darcy pulling her closer.

Lizzy giggled, and hugged him back. 'I am happier even than Jane; she only smiles, I laugh.'

Recognising the words from their favourite book, Darcy dissolved into laughter. 'And I cannot wait to spend the rest of my life in love and laughter with you, my dearest, loveliest Elizabeth!'

About the Author

Jane Odiwe is the author of seven Austen-inspired books, *Mr Darcy's Christmas Calendar*, *Mrs Darcy's Diamonds*, *Project Darcy*, *Searching for Captain Wentworth*, *Mr Darcy's Secret*, *Willoughby's Return*, and *Lydia Bennet's Story*.

Recent television appearances include a *Masterchef* Special, celebrating 200 years of *Sense and Sensibility*, and an interview for the 200 year anniversary of *Pride and Prejudice* on *BBC Breakfast*.

Jane is a member of the Jane Austen Society; she holds an arts degree, and initially started her working life teaching Art and History. With her husband, children, and two cats, Jane divides her time between North London, and Bath, England. When she's not writing, she enjoys painting and trying to capture the spirit of Jane Austen's world. Her illustrations have been published in a picture book, *Effusions of Fancy*, and are featured in a biographical film of Jane Austen's life in Sony's DVD edition of *The Jane Austen Book Club*.

Website: http://austeneffusions.com
Blog: http://janeaustensequels.blogspot.co.uk
Austen Variations: http://austenvariations.com
White Soup Press: http://whitesouppress.com
Facebook: http//facebook.com/JaneOdiwe
Twitter: @JaneOdiwe

Other Books by *Jane Odiwe*

Miss Darcy's Parisian Pin - A new novella in the Jane Austen Jewel Box series, continuing Georgiana's story after the conclusion of Mrs Darcy's Diamonds. **Spring 2015**

Mrs Darcy's Diamonds

Elizabeth is newly married to Fitzwilliam Darcy, the richest man in Derbyshire, landowner of a vast estate, and master of Pemberley House. Elizabeth's new role is daunting at first, and having to deal with Mr Darcy's aunt, Lady Catherine de Bourgh, is a daily challenge. But, Elizabeth is deeply in love and determined to rise to every test and trial she is forced to endure. When her husband presents her with a diamond ring, part of the precious and irreplaceable Darcy suite of jewels, she feels not only honoured and secure in her husband's love, but also ready to accept her new responsibilities and position.

Elizabeth knows she will face exacting scrutiny at the approaching Christmas Ball, but it will be her chance to prove that she is a worthy mistress, and she is excited to be playing hostess to the Bennets, the Bingleys, and the gentry families of Derbyshire, as well as Mr Darcy's French cousins. Antoine de Valois and his sister Louise have arrived at the invitation of Lady Catherine de Bourgh and Elizabeth is delighted that this young and lively couple are helping to bring Miss Georgiana Darcy out of her shell. However, when her ring goes missing before the ball, Elizabeth is distraught, and her dilemma further increased by the threat of a scandal that appears to involve the French cousins.

Project Darcy

It is high summer when Ellie Bentley joins an archaeological dig at Jane Austen's childhood home. She's always had a talent for 'seeing' into the past and is not easily disturbed by her encounters with Mr Darcy's ghost at the house where she's staying.

When Ellie travels into the past she discovers exactly what happened whilst Jane danced her way through the snowy winter of 1796 with her dashing Irish friend. As Steventon Rectory and all its characters come to life, Ellie discovers the true love story lost in Pride and Prejudice – a tale which has its own consequences for her future destiny, changing her life beyond imagination.

Searching for Captain Wentworth

When aspiring writer Sophie Elliot receives the keys to the family townhouse in Bath, it's an invitation she can't turn down, especially when she learns that she will be living next door to the house where Jane Austen lived. On discovering that an ancient glove belonging to her mysterious neighbour, Josh Strafford, will transport her back in time to Regency Bath, she questions her sanity, but Sophie is soon caught up in two dimensions, each reality as certain as the other. Torn between her life in the modern world and that of her ancestor who befriends Jane Austen and her fascinating brother Charles, Sophie's story travels two hundred years across time and back again, to unite this modern heroine with her own Captain Wentworth. Blending fact and fiction together, the tale of Jane Austen's own quest for happiness weaves alongside, creating a believable world of new possibilities for the inspiration behind Persuasion.

Mr Darcy's Secret

After capturing the heart of the most eligible bachelor in England, Elizabeth Bennet believes her happiness is complete-until the day she unearths a stash of anonymous, passionate love letters that may be Darcy's, and she realizes just how little she knows about the guarded, mysterious man she married... Mr Darcy's Secret is a story about love and misunderstandings; of overcoming doubt and trusting to the real feelings of the heart - Elizabeth and the powerful, compelling figure of Mr Darcy take centre stage in this romantic tale set in Regency Derbyshire and the Lakes, alongside the beloved characters from Pride and Prejudice.

Willoughby's Return

In Jane Austen's Sense and Sensibility, when Marianne Dashwood marries Colonel Brandon, she puts her heartbreak over dashing scoundrel John Willoughby in the past. Three years later, Willoughby's return throws Marianne into a tizzy of painful memories and exquisite feelings of uncertainty. Willoughby is as charming, as roguish, and as much in love with her as ever. And the timing couldn't be worse—with Colonel Brandon away and Willoughby determined to win her back, will Marianne find the strength to save her marriage, or will the temptation of a previous love be too powerful to resist?

Lydia Bennet's Story

In Lydia Bennet's Story we are taken back to Jane Austen's most beloved novel, Pride and Prejudice, to a Regency world seen through Lydia's eyes where pleasure and marriage are the only pursuits. But the road to matrimony is fraught with difficulties and even when she is convinced that she has met the man of her dreams, complications arise. When Lydia is reunited with the Bennets, Bingleys, and Darcys for a grand ball at Netherfield Park, the shocking truth about her husband may just cause the greatest scandal of all...

Reviews

Mrs Darcy's Diamonds
Mrs Darcy's Diamonds gives readers a peek into Darcy and Elizabeth's happily ever after, showing the depths of their passion without getting too steamy and how the strength of their love will enable them to conquer any challenge thrown at them. Odiwe does a great job packing a lot into such a short story so that I was never bored, nor did I feel overwhelmed.
DIARY OF AN ECCENTRIC

Project Darcy
Odiwe writes with great charm and assurance: her contemporary characters are engaging, her historical protagonists convincing. In Project Darcy she takes a slice of literary history and turns it into a thoroughly entertaining, often very funny, and frequently touching piece of modern romantic fiction.
JANE AUSTEN'S REGENCY WORLD MAGAZINE

Searching for Captain Wentworth
Searching for Captain Wentworth will send you on a magical journey through time, and your heart, that you will not soon forget -
AUSTENPROSE

Mr Darcy's Secret
Jane Odiwe comes to it steeped in Austen, in all her renditions; Odiwe's sentences often glint with reflections of the great Jane …
HISTORICAL NOVEL SOCIETY

Willoughby's Return
Odiwe's elegantly stylish writing is seasoned with just the right dash of tart humour, and her latest literary endeavour is certain to delight both Austen devotees and Regency romance readers
BOOKLIST

Lydia Bennet's Story

Odiwe pays nice homage to Austen's stylings and endears the reader to the formerly secondary character, spoiled and impulsive Lydia Bennet ... devotees will enjoy

PUBLISHER'S WEEKLY